MARSHALL CAVENDISH CLASSICS

THEY DO RETURN ... BUT GENTLY LEAD THEM BACK

They Do Return… But Gently Lead Them Back

CATHERINE LIM

First published in 1983 by Times Editions

This edition published in 2021 by Marshall Cavendish Editions
An imprint of Marshall Cavendish International

Other Marshall Cavendish Offices:
Marshall Cavendish Corporation, 800 Westchester Ave, Suite N-641, Rye Brook, NY 10573, USA • Marshall Cavendish International (Thailand) Co Ltd, 253 Asoke, 16th Floor, Sukhumvit 21 Road, Klongtoey Nua, Wattana, Bangkok 10110, Thailand • Marshall Cavendish (Malaysia) Sdn Bhd, Times Subang, Lot 46, Subang Hi-Tech Industrial Park, Batu Tiga, 40000 Shah Alam, Selangor Darul Ehsan, Malaysia

National Library Board, Singapore Cataloguing in Publication Data

Name(s): Lim, Catherine.
Title: They do return ... but gently lead them back / Catherine Lim.
Other title(s): Marshall Cavendish classics.
Description: Singapore : Marshall Cavendish Editions, 2021. | First published in 1983 by Times Editions.
Identifier(s): OCN 1253349643 | ISBN 978-981-4974-47-9 (paperback)
Subject(s): Paranormal fiction. | Superstition--Fiction.
Classification: DDC S823--dc23

Printed in Singapore

Contents

The Old Man in the Balcony

One of my earliest recollections is of an immense coffin – perhaps the immensity was derived from the child's perception of the world from her tiny, three-foot frame, for I could not have been more than four then – standing in a covered part of the stone courtyard of a very old house. The coffin had been bought by the mistress of the house for her father-in-law, who had reached that hopeless stage of senility of having to be fed and bathed like a child.

I could still see him clearly – a very old man with long white, wispy hair and beard, crouching in a corner of the balcony upstairs, wearing a kind of faded coat, but naked from the waist down. Occasionally, his daughter-in-law would squat down with scissors and patiently trim his hair, beard and fingernails.

We children used to stare wonderingly at him whenever we were brought on a visit to the house. After the coffin, the old man with no trousers was a natural attraction, and we stood in a cluster just beyond the doorway, staring at him, but at the same time poised for flight should he spring up and attempt to catch us. Of course he was incapable of doing anything apart from eating soft food and soiling himself, but still we associated him with a large fund of supernatural strength that he could always draw upon to attack and kill people.

The coffin had been in readiness for the last 20 years, but the old man lingered on, and his daughter-in-law, whom I remember we called 'Ah Han Chare,' had clearly quite forgotten about its existence or had chosen to ignore it as she went about her business of being the town's matchmaker and bridal helper. She was a jovial, friendly woman who laughed a great deal, and even at that age I remember I was struck by the contrast between her effervescence, her merry laughter and her bright jangling jewels, and the desolate coffin now beginning to gather dust and cobwebs, that had become a fixture in her house. That she had bought it for her father-in-law was a measure of her great affection for him.

At some time in their old age, men and women fretted about the possibility of dying without a proper coffin to be buried in. To reassure her father-in-law that no such calamity would befall him. Ah Han Chare had bought him the coffin, and from that moment he had ceased to fret and worry.

"My mother-in-law was a mean, cruel woman, but he has always been good to me," said Ah Han Chare, explaining this filial gesture. The coffin had stood for so long in the house that soon it lost all its terror for the children in the household. They played around it, and when no one was looking, tried to lift its heavy lid and slip inside.

On the night the coffin knockings began, Ah Han Chare and Ah Kum Soh, a distant relative who was staying with her, sat up in their beds, listened intently and nodded to each other.

"It will be soon," they said. "The signs are here already." And they thought, without sadness, of the deliverance of the old man curled asleep on a mat in the room next to the balcony, a place grown musty and foul-smelling with urine and dropped food. They listened for a while and counted the knocks, all 17 of them.

"Perhaps it will be tomorrow," said Ah Kum Soh. When morning came, she padded softly to the old man's room, but he was clearly still alive, for he looked at her with his bleary eyes and signalled that he wanted to be carried to his warm sunny spot in the corner of the balcony.

In the afternoon, someone rushed to Ah Han Chare and said, "He's dead!" But he was referring to Ah Kum Soh's husband, an idle good-for-nothing wastrel who wandered through the town all day in singlet and pyjama trousers, picking his teeth. The man had fallen into a drain and died there. There was a deep gash on his head and he had apparently been dead a few hours before being spotted by a passing trishaw man. Ah Kum Soh became hysterical and put the blame of her husband's death squarely on the old man in the balcony.

"The coffin knockings were meant for him," she wept, "but he did not want to go, so my husband had to go instead. You mark my words, there will be more deaths yet!"

When the coffin knockings were heard once more, Ah Han Chare and Ah Kum Soh again sat up and listened intently. The knocks came distinctly in the middle of the night – *knock, knock, knock* — becoming more and more faint until they were finally absorbed into the stillness of the night.

Ah Kum Son's son, a frail little asthmatic child of seven, had a fainting fit and was rushed to hospital. He did not die, but the whole town – which by this time had heard of the mysterious knockings at night, and which was talking about Ah Kum Soh's husband's death in awed whispers – started rumours about a small corpse being brought home, and of another of the relatives about to die, in response to the coffin's call.

"Why doesn't the old man answer the call?" they asked. "How many must go in his place?" Ah Kum Soh, weeping, stood before the old man as he was crouching half-naked on the balcony, and began to berate him for his heinous crime. He stared at her, eyes grey and rheumy, and once or twice he looked around and called pathetically, "Ah Han! Ah Han!" for his daughter-in-law's name was the only one he could call now.

Ah Han Chare fell ill shortly after, and the town was gripped with tense expectation. The coffin had called again, impatient to have an occupant after the long years of waiting, and now it was the mistress of the household herself. I remember the anxiety communicated to us children, for we did not venture near the coffin any more, nor look at the old man whose stubborn refusal to answer the coffin knockings resulted in the tragic deaths of others.

A priest from the town temple was called in to appease the coffin and persuade it to end its persistent calls, for the knockings had persisted for several nights. Ah Han Chare lay in a stupor, surrounded by weeping children and relatives.

"Ah Han! Ah Han!" came the whimperings from the old man, hungry and terrified, for in the days of confusion following her sudden illness, he had neither been washed nor fed. Nobody heard him.

On the fourth day, a child ran in to announce: "He's dead! He's dead! I saw him myself! He's all stiff and there are ants in his eyes too!" They went to see, and true enough, he was dead, fallen on his side, his thin legs doubled up under him.

They rejoiced to see Ah Han Chare out of danger.

She was able to sit up in bed and take a bowl of porridge. The knockings ceased, the old man was laid in the coffin and buried next to his wife, who had died 30 years earlier.

Ah Han Chare, when it was all over, was able to speak about the coffin knockings as if they had been everyday occurrences, it being part of her exuberant nature to be able to weave the coffin incidents into the ribald tales she invariably carried away with her after the wedding festivities that she organized with much zest. But her popularity as matchmaker and bridal helper declined sharply, for she became connected with coffin knocks, and few were prepared to risk the taint of death in a house of marriage.

A Boy Named Ah Mooi

I was so used to calling my playmate 'Ah Mooi' that it took me years to realize that 'Ah Mooi' was really a name suitable for girls. But by then it was too late to ask him why, for the expansiveness of childhood had narrowed into the awkward tentativeness of adolescence. And the tiny gold earring that his mother made him wear on his left ear – that had never struck me as odd.

I don't suppose he is called Ah Mooi now – his real name translates into something like Prosperous Dragon-Lord – or wears the gold earring. I wonder whether he remembers the story of the time when the devils, in their insane jealousy, nearly caused his death?

His mother, frantic with fear, had consulted the temple medium who immediately went into a trance and said that the devils would stop tormenting the baby boy only if they could be deceived into believing that he was not a male child.

Male children, treasured by their parents and grandparents and doted on, were objects of intense jealousy of the evil spirits; female children, being considerably less valued, were left alone. So Prosperous

Dragon-Lord from that day was called Ah Mooi. To make doubly sure that the spirits would be deceived into believing that he was a common, useless female child, his mother had made him wear the gold earring on one ear.

The deception must have been totally successful, for Ah Mooi grew up strong and sturdy and was seldom ill. I remember that as a very small child, he sweated under a multitude of vests, shirts and a jacket but was allowed to run bare-bottomed. And it was in later years that I wondered at the stupidity of fiends who could be deceived into believing he was female when there was such explicit proof to the contrary. Ah Mooi had four older sisters. The girls were nothing in the eyes of his parents and grandparents; he was everything, being a male child.

Throughout his childhood, he was protected, with ferocious dedication by the whole household, against the evil spirits which were everywhere. One of his sisters, a talkative feather-brained girl, once made a comment on his plumpness and healthy appetite as she was watching him being fed. She was immediately slapped across the mouth and warned that any more such foolish invitation of the jealous spirits to come and harm the child would entail a punishment even more severe. Fortunately for her, Ah Mooi did not fall ill after that or lose his appetite, and she was never again guilty of the folly of openly praising her baby brother.

Ah Mooi fell near a large stone in a piece of waste ground that the servant girl had taken him to; when he had a fever the next day, the servant girl was dismissed and Lau Ah Sim, a pious old woman in the neighbourhood, was called upon to conduct the propitiatory ritual at the spot where Ah Mooi had fallen.

I had never seen any of these rituals in my life, though I often saw, usually by roadsides, signs that they had taken place – reel candles, joss-sticks and once a small mirror. Lau Ah Sim was always performing them for the neighbourhood children who had fallen ill. In an old, quavering voice, Lau Ah Sim, I was told, chanted prayers to placate the evil spirits and to request that they leave the child in peace.

Round Ah Mooi's neck must have been a whole armoury of amulets and charms against these dreadful beings – I remember seeing little metal cylinders and triangular pieces of yellow cloth with some words on them. He also wore a tiger's claw surrounded by a delicate band of gold and a jade bracelet: these purported to ward off evil influences. Thus securely protected, Ah Mooi went through a healthy childhood, and at some stage, his parents must have felt that he had passed the danger period and could now afford to doff name, gold earring and amulets.

Although mere females, Ah Mooi's sisters must

have been valued enough for their parents not to want to take any chances with the evil spirits, for they were given such names as 'Bad Smell', 'Pig', and 'Dumb', although their registered names were redolent of the best of oriental virtues and treasures.

One of them – I think it was Bad Smell – was often sickly as a child. The reason was that her destiny and her mother's were ill-matched; in fact, they clashed violently. So Bad Smell had to call her mother 'Aunt' and her father 'Uncle', and once again, evil forces were deceived and their work undone.

What did they look like – these much feared spirits that infested the air, the trees, grassy mounds, stones and every cranny of the house? I had never thought much about their appearances until I saw a mirror hanging over the doorway of a relative's house and was told that it was there to keep the evil spirits away. Thus the fiend, upon reaching the doorway, would not fail to see its reflection in the mirror, and be so alarmed by its own grotesque appearance that it would immediately disappear from the premises.

I thought that this was an extremely clever plan to get rid of evil spirits and, for a while, my imagination dwelt long on the image of a hairy, large-eyed creature with fangs (an impression derived solely from the cheap comic books that I was beginning to devour) sailing through the air and suddenly stopping short in front of the mirror above the doorway, staring incredulously at the ugly visage, and then making a quick about-turn with a howl of anguish.

Ah Mooi survived the evil; Ah Khoon did not.

Like Ah Mooi, Ah Khoon was the longed-for male child after several daughters. His mother, despised by her mother-in-law for being able to bring forth only female children, swore to the Nine Deities that if she had a male child, she would go to the temple for the Feast of the Nine Deities every year and show her gratitude by fasting and taking part in the tongue-skewing ceremony.

Ah Khoon was born a sickly, puny baby, not expected to live. But his mother, her confinement hardly over, went to the temple to offer prayers and gifts of gratitude to the Nine Deities. That was the cause often brought up to account for the poor health of the child and his eventual sad end, for she was still in her confinement and therefore impure when she went before the presence of the Nine Deities. She should never have committed the sacrilege. That negated all future acts of propitiation, so it was useless for her to have taken part in the tongue-skewing ceremony. She was the first woman in the town's history to do so; the deities were probably not pleased, for she developed ulcers on her tongue when there should have been no skewer mark.

Desperate when Ah Khoon developed asthma, she consulted a temple medium who prescribed herbal cures that probably contained a high percentage of arsenic. For years Ah Khoon was given this herbal mixture over which the temple medium always chanted prayers before he sold it in packets to Ah Khoon's mother.

One morning the boy was found dead, and his mother, overcome with grief, unleashed a torrent of abuse at the deities who had played her out so cruelly. She was stopped by the scandalized relatives who feared more harm would come to the unfortunate family.

Ah Mooi's mother, who generously rendered help during those trying days, was secretly convinced that had Ah Khoon's mother taken the simple precaution of changing his name to a girl's instead of doing those useless, crazy things at the Temple of the Nine Deities, he would have lived.

The Legacy

Ah Hoe Peh was my grandfather's opium '*kaki*'. A *kaki* was, in a sense, more than a friend. Without *kaki*, the pleasures of certain activities such as opium-smoking, durian-eating and mahjong-playing were considerably diminished or rendered impossible. With *kaki*, it was likely for one to reach the zenith of these pleasures.

Grandfather, Ah Hoe Peh and some other *kaki* smoked opium for hours in grandfather's room or sometimes in Ah Hoe Peh's room. From the outside, you can hear nothing save the bubbling of the opium liquid in the cups of the bamboo pipes; if you'd peeped inside, you'd have seen the men lugubriously reclining on their mats and inhaling the opium, a languorous look in their eyes. Both men had been smoking opium from their youth. Grandfather, it was rumoured, had spent a large part of grandmother's dowry to support the habit.

Ah Hoe Peh did likewise with his wife's jewels, and when these were gone, he had managed to beg or borrow, for the profits from his small dry-goods business were barely sufficient to bring up his four sons.

All the boys went to school; it was to the credit of

Ah Hoe Chim that she never allowed her sons to go hungry, or be humiliated in school because they could not pay their school fees. As for herself, she ate plain rice with warm water, sometimes a few pieces of vegetable. For a time, she helped grandmother sew beaded bridal slippers for a small payment.

Ah Hoe Chim, thin and dry as a stick, outlived her husband by many years, but never enjoyed the rich legacy that he had promised to leave (but which in fact he did, according to his sons, who were only too willing to indulge their father's expensive habit once they had started working and bringing money home).

"I'm leaving a rich legacy, you'll see," Ah Hoe Peh had said time and again, "and it will be more than Soon Huat's rubber and coconut plantations and shophouses," alluding to the enormous wealth that the town's only millionaire had left behind for innumerable wives, children and grandchildren to squabble over.

Ah Hoe Chim clucked her tongue with impatience and skepticism; she always did when her husband spoke of the legacy. But she was not a quarrelsome woman and said nothing, preferring to spend her time and energy supervising her sons while they were doing their homework by the light of the oil-lamp, and knocking her knuckles on their heads if she thought they were wasting their time. Never educated herself, she believed wholeheartedly in the value of education and would soundly discipline any child if he got a bad report from school. When she caught them listening to their father's idle tales, she shooed them back to their books, to which they would return with wry faces.

"I'm leaving my sons, and my sons' sons a rich legacy," said Ah Hoe Peh. When the doctor diagnosed his disease as terminal cancer of the stomach, he became more urgent about this promise and the means to ensure that it was fulfilled. He had to give up his opium in the last weeks before his death; surprisingly, there was little pain in spite of the ravages of the disease, due, according to his sons, to the numbing effects of the opium over the years. Wasted to a skeleton, but urged on by his anxiety to keep his promise of leaving behind a rich legacy – an urge that was daily becoming stronger with the approach of death – he managed to drag himself to consult the temple medium.

"At what time will I die?" he wanted to know. The medium assured him it would be very early in the morning, well before the first meal of the day. But he was not satisfied. He wanted to be certain that, it would not be in the evening, when all three meals of the clay would have been eaten, when therefore no legacy would be left. For a man would have eaten up everything and left nothing for his sons, and his sons' sons. A considerate man had to die in the morning, never in the evening.

Ah Hoe Peh went into his death throes in the evening, his wife and sons gathered around him and watched as he struggled to make it to the morning. The death rattle was already in his throat; his eyes were already unseeing, but still Ah Hoe Peh fought to stave off death, to keep it at bay till the clock strike and announce the hour of dawn. As the first faint cock-crow quavered in the cold night air and reached the dying man's ears, he smiled at his triumph and the bequeathing of a legacy that would be enduring.

For years, his family spoke about the old man's heroic efforts to stay alive till the moment when the fulfilment of his promise could be assured. His sons later made good. One of them is a millionaire, and his millions, he says with profound gratitude, are the three meals of the day that were selflessly left uneaten.

The Story of Father Monet

Were they ghosts? Had I actually seen ghosts?

Indian labourers, someone had ventured – perhaps an Indian labourer and his wife hacking grass beside the church. But they were not Indian, I insisted. The man was definitely a European, dressed like a priest, and the woman was Chinese. A trick of the imagination; someone else had proffered the stereotypical explanation for ghosts. But it could not be, I countered, for at that time I had no knowledge whatsoever of the French priest and the Chinese woman who was one of his parishioners. It was only later that I came to hear of it. It would have been the rarest of coincidences for my imagination to have given birth to three such characters – the man, the woman and the baby in the bundle she was carrying – that coincided in every detail with the characters of that tragedy which took place years before I was born.

I have been puzzling over this since and have come to the conclusion that the three I saw that day were ghosts. Some people also claimed to have seen them, sometimes together, sometimes separately. The one who had seen them most often, it was rumoured, was the Chinese woman's husband, who lived a year after his wife and who was plagued with bad dreams almost to the very last day of his life. He was the cause of all the suffering, it was said, and it was fitting that he should die in an agony of madness and fear for his terrible injustice.

Nobody seemed to remember their names, so they shall be given fictitious ones.

Father Monet was a Catholic priest from France, possibly one of the first to be sent to this part of the world. He was an active, dedicated man of God who quickly settled down to his new life in the new country and almost immediately began looking around for converts. Coupled with his aggressive missionary zeal, however, was a warm humanity and an instinctive understanding of people that quickly won him the trust of many. He mastered Hokkien after only a few months, and spent much time among his parishioners, preaching to them, saying the rosary with them or simply being a willing listener. He was a handsome man, tall and fair-skinned, with a dark luxuriant beard and light blue eyes which exuded a natural warmth.

The Lai family always welcomed Father Monet into their home to talk to them or share a meal with them. They were devout Catholics; they boasted of being third-generation Catholics, and their forebears had been among the first to be converted by missionaries in China.

The elder Lai had a thriving wholesale business in rice, coffee powder and certain brands of milk powder. It would eventually be inherited by his son, a young man of about 25. The younger Lai was a hard-working, intelligent man, but given to bouts of sullen temper and depression. His parents easily diagnosed the cause to be the want of a wife and, trusting Father Monet's judgment more than the town matchmaker's, enjoined him to look for a wife for their son.

The request had a very specific object: The family knew that Father Monet was in the habit of visiting another Catholic family, comprising a humble tailor, his wife and their very beautiful and shy daughter who had been given the name Mary Anna Joseph at baptism. The elder Lai and his wife had decided upon Mary for their daughter-in-law. Their son appeared not to protest when she was mentioned, and that was encouragement enough for the elderly couple, who had despaired of ever finding a bride acceptable to their sullen, silent, hot-tempered son.

Father Monet dutifully approached Mary's parents who, in their simplicity and humility, expressed immense gratitude and hoped the marriage would take place as soon as possible. But as for Mary, Father Monet could get neither word nor look from her to indicate her true feelings. Her face retained the very serene, placid expression it always wore; her lips remained shut when Father Monet asked, "And what about you, Mary? What do you say to the offer?"

Mary continued to pour out the tea for Father Monet, her eyes modestly lowered. She served him some rice cakes, but all that time not a word escaped her lips.

Father Monet paused between mouthfuls, looked at her and asked, "Are you not happy, Mary? Lai is a good man and a devout Catholic. He will make you a good husband."

Looking at her closely for the first time, the priest was startled by her loveliness, a loveliness all the more striking for its lack of adornment. The girl wore her hair severely pulled back from her face and coiled at the back; her dress was always the modest long-sleeved samfu, in colours that were surely too drab for her vibrant and blooming youthful beauty.

"Mary, if you don't wish to marry Lai, I will not force you," he said ever so gently. And when her mother began to scold her shrilly for disobedience, he rose from the table to intervene. The girl's eyes filled with tears though she did not once raise her hand to wipe them.

On his next visit, she served him as usual, with eyes downcast. He looked steadily at her and wondered what went on in her mind and heart, this intense, outwardly serene girl-woman. At one point, she looked up briefly to say, not without a certain resoluteness, "I will marry Lai," and then withdrew into her world of silence and private thoughts again. Father Monet was more than a little troubled and wished to speak with her further, to satisfy himself that the girl was not being coerced into a union that was indissoluble in the eyes of God. But she gave the impression that she wanted no more said on the matter.

She married Lai shortly, in the little wooden Catholic church. It became a matter of urgent duty to Father Monet to ascertain that she was happy since he felt partly responsible for her marriage. He continued to visit the Lai home frequently in the first few months. After a while, he was satisfied.

Mary was apparently contented with her lot. The in-laws were very fond of her, and as for Lai, there was no husband who doted more on his wife. It seemed as if a wife were all he needed to get him out of his sullenness and ill temper. His was a possessive, all-consuming love. Never once did he let his beautiful young wife out of his sight. In the openness of the big house which he shared not only with his parents but with his relatives as well, propriety and fear of being laughed at prevented him from always wanting to be close to her, to look at her, to touch her. In the privacy of their room, the largest and most comfortable in the house, there was no more need to rein in the passion and the desire to possess completely.

Father Monet found it most troubling indeed as he watched them while pretending to be absorbed by the food they had laid before him or the antics of the relatives' small children playing nearby, for it could not escape his notice that Mary winced at her husband's every touch and look. It was hardly perceptible, but the shrewd priest saw it all. His immediate reaction was to give Mary a good lecture at his first opportunity about performing her wifely duty.

The opportunity came soon after; it was evening and the priest had come to join in the family rosary. He came a little earlier, and found Mary alone in the sitting-room, mending a tear in her husband's trousers. The sight was somehow rather reassuring to Father Monet, and he began to compliment her on her dutifulness as a wife, unaware that as he went on, she had begun to cry and was already unable to control the tears that fell freely on the garment now lying on her lap.

"Why, Mary, what's the matter? Tell me," he asked in consternation, moving towards her as her sobs gathered into a paroxysm that shook her slight frame. He placed his hands on her shoulders, suddenly full of pity for this strange, gentle woman, so unlike other young women in the town who would have been glad of half her good fortune.

In the ensuing months, he did not see her cry any longer, but did notice her husband's return to his sullenness and peevishness, a natural consequence for a man who, ardently offering love, continually finds it repulsed.

Then began a period of intense jealousy; the younger Lai believing that his wife preferred the white-skinned priest to him. Did she not always want to be the one to serve him the food and drink, although his mother or the relatives could perform the duty just as well? And did she not always somehow find an excuse to come out of her room or the kitchen whenever he came by?

Tortured by such thoughts, he withdrew yet further into his grimness, and watched her, and watched him. Although he could see nothing to torment him further, his mind would not let him rest, but suggested to him dark and direful possibilities. And then, almost like a godsend, his wife became pregnant; a new softness came over her features, and she actually appeared content as she quietly went about her work in the house.

When Lai announced the news to Father Monet, it was in the warm confidentiality of friendship fully restored. He waxed loquacious in the expression of hopes for a boy – the first grandson for the grandparents on both sides. Father Monet was too relieved for words. He left for France shortly after that, giving them the promise that he would return in time to baptize the infant.

The period of waiting was marked by extra visits to church, extra prayers, more works of charity; Lai was ready to take any precaution against mishaps. He engaged the best midwife to attend to his wife, and on the evening of the birth, stood outside the locked door of the room, aware of the footsteps of the midwife inside, the low moans of his wife, the bustling about with basins of hot water and wads of absorbent paper. He waited, tense and quivering, and at the first cry of the child, knocked on the door and fairly shouted, "Is it a boy?"

"It is a boy," said the midwife after a pause.

"Let me come in then," he said, his heart suddenly swelling with joy, and he knocked yet louder, ready to look upon the face of his first-born.

The door was at last opened and he strode in, heart pounding. His wife was lying on the bed, face pale as a ghost. Beside her was the child wrapped in a towel. The midwife stood nearby, her hands still wet with the blood and with such a stricken look on her face that, sensing something amiss, he strode to the bed, flung aside the towel covering the child and then recoiled in horror. The child was all white and pink: its hair was white, its eyes were pink; it was not his. He stood staring at it, speechless. Then he looked at his wife who looked back at him; and then at the midwife who turned away with a sob.

"In all my years as midwife, I have not delivered a child like this."

The pounding in his brain and heart allowed no other feeling except a numbing sensation that something had gone very wrong. When the pounding had ceased sufficiently for other feelings to rush in, rage swelled and took possession with such force that he found himself roaring at the top of his voice and looking around for something to break, to crush and destroy.

The porcelain basin was smashed onto the floor, spilling the water red with the blood. He hit one of the bedposts, smashed a wooden stool against the wall, and yet his anger was not assuaged. Uppermost in his mind was the fact that the priest whom he had trusted and the woman whom he had married and assumed virtuous had betrayed him. The pain would overpower him until he stopped smashing things, broke down and wept into his hands.

The midwife had run out of the room, screaming for help; his wife continued to lie motionless on the bed. And now her look of placidity aroused him to a new pitch of rage, and he began shouting "Whore! Whore!" at her. He wanted to strangle her with his bare hands. Something in her expression prevented him from doing so, and he could only stand at a distance, his half-clenched fingers straining towards her in impotent fury. Suddenly, as if inspired by an idea that would put an end to all the misery, he grabbed the child and ran out of the room.

"Oh, do be careful –" cried his wife, showing agitation for the first time, but he was gone.

With the bundle in his arms, he ran through the darkness of lanes and paths, all the way until he reached the church. He ran to the back where the priest's sleeping quarters were (a tiny room with only a plank bed and a table and chair) and pounded the door furiously with one hand while holding the bundle with the other.

"Open up – open up this very minute!" he gasped. When the priest appeared, blinking uncertainly in the haziness of roused sleep, he pushed in and confronted the priest.

"Take what's yours," he said, thrusting the bundle at the priest. The priest barely had time for an audible gasp before the bundle was flung at him. Fortunately he caught it and discovered, for the first time, that it was a new-born child, naked and beginning to squall.

"What – " he began, his mind still unable to give meaning to the night's strange happening, and then he found himself fighting off blows with his right arm, while he held and protected the baby with his left. The blows were savage, but he could still fight them off and not let any touch the child. But when he saw the wooden chair lifted and descending on him, he sank to the floor and covered the child with both arms as well as his arched body. A terrible pain seemed to explode through his whole body – and then all was, mercifully, darkness.

They later found the child dead in the towel, the priest, battered and soaked with blood. They found Lai in the far corner, taunting the priest with a maniacal glee as he kept repealing, "Take back your bastard! Take back your white-skinned bastard!"

Whether he was sent to prison or not, nobody could quite remember, but it was said his mind had come unhinged, and it seemed his father kept him locked up in a special room at home. Till the end of his days, he could not or would not understand what had happened; even his old mother tried to tell him that the child was his, that in her time she had come across several instances of these poor unfortunate white-skinned children with the white hair and pink eyes, and they were no less loved by their parents. But he would not listen; he would only-shake his head and say, "Whore!" or "A white man's bastard," and "A foreign hairy devil's bastard."

As for Father Monet, the incident left him permanently blind and paralysed. He was to have been sent back to France, but died before arrangements could be made.

Mary returned to her parents, and it was said that she ran to the hospital one night to see the priest, but he was already beyond recognizing anyone. Not only was he blind, but his eardrums had been badly damaged. Rumours arose about there having been something between the French priest and the beautiful Chinese woman who loathed her husband and secretly loved the priest.

The circumstances of Mary's death were shadowy. Some said she died after an illness, some said she killed herself in grief after having seen the priest.

When I passed the church that evening and saw – or thought I saw – the priest, Mary and the child in the bundle – they must have lain in their graves for at least 50 years.

Once, not so long ago, I paid a visit to the modern church that now stands where the old one was, and asked the priest, a very friendly and talkative rosy-cheeked fellow, if he kept records of all the priests who had served in the church, including the old one. He said he did not have any that went as far back as 50 years.

"Is the story of Father Monet true?" I asked. He replied: "I too have heard of the strange story of Father Monet and of people who claimed to have seen his ghost and the other ghosts. But I assure you this church has been blessed with holy water. No ghosts will ever be seen in its precincts."

Grandfather's Story

Grandmother died when I was about 10. I had always been in awe of her, mainly because of the stories I had heard relatives and servants whisper about her atrocities towards the many bondmaids she had bought as infants, and reared to work as seamstresses and needlewomen in her rapidly expanding business of making bridal clothes and furnishings.

Grandmother's embroidered silk bed curtains and bolster cases, and beaded slippers for bride and groom were famous and fetched good money. The more nimble-fingered of the bondmaids did the sewing and beadwork; the others were assigned the less demanding tasks of cutting, pasting, dyeing, stringing beads, or general housework.

It was rumoured that one bondmaid had died from injuries sustained when grandmother flung a durian at her. The story had never been confirmed, and as a child, my imagination had often dwelt on the terrible scene, giving it a number of interesting variations: grandmother hurled the durian at the bondmaid's head and it stuck there; the durian was flung at the bondmaid's stomach, thus disembowelling her; the durian thorns stuck in the bondmaid's flesh like so many knives and caused her to bleed to death.

Whatever the circumstances surrounding her death, the bondmaid was certainly dead at 15 and quietly buried at night in a remote part of the huge plantation in which stood grandmother's house.

Grandfather, who had been separated from grandmother for as long as anyone could remember, often said, "Look at her hands. Look at the strength and power in them. The hands of a murderess." And he would go on to assign the same pernicious quality to each feature of her body: her eyes were cold and glittering, her mouth was thin and cruel, her buttocks which by their flatness deflected all good fortune, so that her husband would always be in want.

I think I unfairly attributed to grandmother all those atrocities which rich elderly ladies of old China committed against their servant girls or their husbands' minor wives and concubines. Thus I had grandmother tie up the ends of the trousers of a bondmaid close to the ankles, force a struggling, clawing cat clown through the opening at the waist, quickly knot the trousers tightly at the waist to trap the beast inside, and then begin to hit it from the outside with a broom so that it would claw and scratch the more viciously in its panic.

I never saw, in the few visits I remember I paid grandmother, any such monstrosity. The punishments that grandmother regularly meted out were less dramatic: she pinched, hit knuckles with a wooden rod, slapped and occasionally rubbed chilli paste against the lips of a child bondmaid who had been caught telling a lie.

Grandmother did not like children. I think she merely tolerated my cousins and me when we went to stay a few days with her. When in a good mood, she gave us some beads or remnants of silk for which she no longer had any use.

I remember asking her one day why I never saw grandfather with her and why he was staying in another house. Not only did she refrain from answering my question but threw me such an angry glare that from that very day I never mentioned grandfather in her hearing. I concluded that they hated each other with a virulence that did not allow each to hear the name of the other without a look of the most intense scorn or words of abuse, spat out rather than uttered.

Indeed, never have I seen a couple so vigorously opposed to each other, and I still wonder how they could have overcome their revulsions to produce three offspring in a row, for according to grandfather, they had hated each other right from the beginning of their marriage. It was probably a duty which grandmother felt she had to discharge.

"It was an arranged marriage," said grandfather simply, "and I never saw her till the wedding night." But he did not speak of the large dowry that grandmother brought with her, for her father was a well-to-do pepper merchant who had businesses in Indonesia. As soon as her parents were dead and she had saved enough money to start a small business on her own, she left grandfather, took up residence in an old house in a plantation that she had shrewdly bought for a pittance, and brought up her three children there. Her two daughters she married off as soon as they reached 16; her son, who turned out to be a wastrel, she left to do as he liked.

She had put her life with grandfather behind her; from that day, he was dead to her, and she pursued her business with single-minded purpose and fervour, getting rich very quickly. She had a canny business sense and invested wisely in rubber and coconut plantations.

Grandfather took up residence with a mistress; he had her for a very long time, almost from the time of his marriage. It was said that she was barren, and he was disappointed for a while, for he wanted sons by her, but his love remained unchanged.

There were other mistresses, but they were merely the objects for grandfather's insatiable appetite, while this woman, a very genteel-looking, soft-spoken woman whom I remember we all called 'Grand aunt', was his chosen life companion. I saw her only once. She was already very old and grey, and I remember she took out a small bottle of pungent-smelling oil from her blouse pocket and rubbed a little under my nose when she saw me cough and sniffle. She died some three years before grandfather (and a year after grandmother).

Grandfather howled in his grief at grand aunt's funeral, and was inconsolable for months. In all likelihood, he would not have attended grandmother's funeral even if she had not objected. As it was, she had stipulated, on her death-bed, that on no condition was grandfather to be allowed near her dead body. She was dying from a terrible cancer that, over a year, ate away her body.

"Go, you must go," urged grand aunt on the day of the funeral, "for in death, all is forgotten." But grandfather lay in his room smoking his opium pipe and gazing languorously up at the ceiling.

When grand aunt died – quite suddenly, for she was taking the chamber pot up to their room when she slipped, fell down the stairs and died – grandfather was grief-stricken and at one point, even blamed the sudden death on grandmother's avenging spirit. He became withdrawn and reticent, and sometimes wept with the abandon of a child in the silence of the night.

The change was marked, for grandfather was by nature garrulous and, on occasion, even jovial. He liked to tell stories – especially irreverently obscene tales of monks. In his withdrawn state, all storytelling ceased, except on one occasion when he emerged from his room, to the surprise of the relatives who were sitting around idly chatting after dinner, and offered to tell a tale.

"Once upon a time," said grandfather, grey eyes misting over and the wispy beard on his thin chin (which he always tied up tightly with a rubber band, much to the amusement of us children) moving up and down with the effort of story-telling.

"A very long time ago, perhaps a thousand years ago, there lived in China a farmer and his wife. He loved her dearly, for she was a gentle, loving woman who would do anything to make him comfortable and happy. They had no children; the woman's barrenness, which would have compelled any husband to reject her, did not in the least irk him. He worked hard to save for their old age, knowing no sons would be born to look after them, and he and his wife watched with satisfaction the silver coins growing in the old stone jar, which they took care to hide in a hole in the earthen floor.

"Now near the farm was a nunnery, and the head nun, a most cruel and mercenary woman who spent all her time thinking of how much in donations she could get out of the simple peasants, began to eye the growing wealth of this farmer and his wife. She knew that they were an extremely frugal couple and surmised that their savings were a goodly sum.

"Knowing that the farmer was a shrewd fellow who regarded her with deep suspicion, she waited one morning for him to be out in the fields before paying his wife a visit.

"So convincing was she in her promise of heavenly blessings upon those who would donate generously to her nunnery that the farmer's wife was quite taken in. The foolish woman went to the hiding place in the earthen floor, brought out the stone jar and handed it, with its store of silver coins within, to the head nun. The nun thanked her effusively and left.

"When the farmer came back, his wife told him what had happened, in her extreme naivete expecting him to praise her for what she had done. Instead, he picked up his *changkul* and repeatedly hit her in his rage. When he saw that she was dead, his rage turned into an overpowering pity and he knew he would never be at peace until he had killed the one who had brought about this tragedy.

"He ran to the nunnery with his changkul and there struck three hefty blows on the nun's head until she fell down and died. In his panic, the farmer ran to a tree and hanged himself.

"The spirits of the three deceased then appeared

before the Almighty, who sat on his heavenly throne in judgment.

"'You have done great wrong,' he told the farmer, 'and must therefore be punished.'

"'You,' turning to the nun. 'have done greater wrong, for you are a selfish, mercenary, cruel woman. You too will be punished.'

"He looked at the farmer's wife and, whereas his eyes had narrowed in severe censure when they looked upon the farmer and the nun, they now softened upon the gentle, timid woman.

"'You are a good woman,' said the Almighty, 'and although you were foolish enough to be taken in by this nun, you will not be punished.'

"The Almighty's plan was simple.

"'I'm sending the three of you back to earth again,' said the Almighty. 'You will be born and at the appointed time, you,' pointing to the farmer, 'and you,' pointing to the nun, 'will be man and wife so that you will be each other's torment. I can devise no greater punishment for you. Since your sin is less,' he continued, addressing the farmer, 'you will be freed of the retribution after a time and will be reunited with this woman, without whom you cannot be happy.'

"Then turning to the nun, he told her, 'You have been guilty of so much cruelty that your punishment will be extended further. While this man and this woman enjoy peace and happiness together, your body will be wracked by the most painful disease, which will, after a long time, carry you to your grave.'

"So the three were reborn on earth, and the Almighty's plans for them came to pass."

Grandfather finished his story and shuffled back to his room, smoking his opium pipe. He paused, before entering his room, to continue, "The woman, much beloved by the man, was to die soon, and he will shortly follow. For them, there will no longer be the pain of another rebirth."

Of Moles and Buttocks

Fourth Aunt-on-father's-side led a sorrowful life and was ill-treated by her irresponsible, lecherous husband because of a mole situated close to her left eye. Second Aunt-on-mother's-side, on the other hand, enjoyed prosperity all her life and was always seen with a heavy gold chain round her neck and a stack of gold bangles round her wrist because of her very substantial buttocks. Poor Fourth Aunt-on-father's-side, in addition to the unfortunate mole near her eye, had flat, truncated buttocks which she blamed more than the mole for her sad life.

As a child, I expertly explained the fortunes or misfortunes of relatives and neighbours in terms of their physiognomy. I had picked up a valuable store of information on the matter from adult conversations and observations, and could, at the age of 10 or thereabouts, look pityingly upon a face that had moles near the eye. I supposed that it must have been because moles near the eyes reminded people of tears and tears meant sorrow.

I rejoiced having a mole near the mouth; by the same token, a mole near the mouth meant that food was always at hand, that the person would never starve. It was better for a woman if the location were close to one side of the upper lip; that meant she would be the concubine of a rich, pampering man and would never be in want for the rest of her days.

Fourth Aunt-on-father's-side's mole was a particularly large one; it hung – round, black and grotesque – between her nose and eye, and I sometimes wondered if, had somebody just twisted it off, would her fortunes change for the better?

Her husband beat her continually, especially when he got drunk; her brood of children were, like herself, timid and silent and resentful. The mole – the mole that was causing all this – couldn't it be removed somehow? I had the vague impression that moles could not be tampered with. They were the seal of judgment of some mighty power, and to try to remove them was to invite the wrath of this power.

After some time, I gave up the hope of Aunt's mole falling off by itself, and the almost daily witnessing of the cruel hardships and privations she was subjected to convinced me that to have a mole near the eye was the saddest thing that could happen.

The buttocks could have overcome the evil effects of the mole, but poor Aunt, although not thin, had extremely flat, fleshless buttocks.

Now a woman, it was ordained, must have round

fleshy buttocks if she were to bring good luck to her husband and enjoy prosperity herself. Grandfather used to complain that he never got rich because Grandmother had unfortunate buttocks; since she enjoyed relative prosperity in her bridal-wear business, I could only come to the conclusion that other lucky features of her physiognomy must have successfully cancelled out the perfidy of the flat buttocks.

But poor Aunt had no redeeming feature. The elderly relatives had been heard to comment, sadly, on her thin lips, her manner of walk in which her feet pointed outwards – a really unfortunate thing! Whatever wealth was coming was always being pushed away – her low narrow forehead, the failure of the tip of her little finger to extend beyond the last joint line of the finger next to it. Crossing this line signified the overcoming of a most crucial life hurdle, and Aunt had again failed in this. Some people tried to make up for this deficiency by letting the fingernail on the little finger grow long enough to extend beyond this fateful line, but Aunt had never bothered to do that.

I remember that on one of the rare occasions when she joked and laughed – even then, the sad pinched look never left her face so that when she laughed, the lines gathered in a rictus that was quite frightening to see – she took me aside, patted me on the buttocks and commented that unlike hers, mine would see me through life smoothly and would I remember her once I became the concubine or wife of a rich man?

Second Aunt-on-mother's-side, who was enormously fat, always found difficulty in getting up from the low cane chair that she used to sit in outside her house after dinner, picking her teeth and chatting amiably with the neighbours. She had extremely fleshy buttocks; I thought they made her look grotesque, but was ready to concede that if they had brought in all those heavy solid gold chains and stacks of gold bangles and goodness knows what else hidden in her jewellery box, there should be little reason to regret them.

It was debatable whether the prosperity came from her buttocks or her husband's, for he too was very prominent in that feature. Although he was by no means fat, the protuberance was most pronounced, and husband and wife taking a leisurely walk side by side on an evening, viewed from behind, would provoke much envy with regard to the double share of Fate's favours.

As if still dissatisfied with inflicting Fourth Aunt's body with a whole range of unfortunate features, Fate had gone on to wreak more vengeance by making her marry a man who had numerous moles on his ears. Fourth Uncle's left ear, I remember being told, was strewn with moles, some quite large, some small and indistinct. This was the surest mark of a faithless husband, a lecher and a scoundrel. Aunt swore that when they were first married, there were no moles on his ear; they seemed to have appeared at a critical period early on in their married life.

Much of Aunt's suffering stemmed not so much from Uncle's womanizing, as from the fact that he had no money left to give her after it. Violent quarrels ensued. Often, Aunt, miserable and humiliated, sent her children around the neighbourhood to borrow rice or sugar or coffee.

Uncle, after a drink or two, sometimes grew expansive and called his terrified children to come around him, talking to them all the time with good-natured garrulousness.

"We are poor," he said with a chuckle, "because of your mother's buttocks – see how flat and useless they are – and because of the moles on my ear. But then, you know, I can't help being what I am."

Full Moon

The full moon, startlingly luminous in the night sky and linked, in the child's mind, with fairy maidens who played on magic flutes and bathed in silver streams, invited the small forefinger to point to it, so that others too might see and comment on its wondrous beauty.

My forefinger was slapped down immediately, and then, remembering what I ought not to have forgotten, hid my hand fearfully in the folds of my dress.

"Do you want your ear cut off?" cried my older, wiser companion. "Have you forgotten Ah Hee?" I remembered Ah Hee well. His right ear was almost falling off; an infection was ravaging it and threatening to sever it from his head. The grocer's boy had pointed to a full moon.

I went to sleep with a hand on each ear and was relieved, the next morning, to find that no such fate had befallen. In my dream afterwards, the full moon, large and vengeful, converted itself into a gigantic metal disc, approached me, and turned its cutting edge towards my right ear so that I screamed and woke.

A nervous child, my elders said, and a triangular piece of yellow cloth with some prayer words sewn onto it was given me to wear. Sweat-stained, food-soiled, the amulet rested comfortably against my chest for the greater part of childhood.

The hospital with its outhouse for the insane was not far from our house. I was brought along on several occasions, when the elders visited sick relatives or friends. A woman who had once worked as a servant for us was in the outhouse for the insane, and from time to time she was allowed out of the barred cells for she was reasonably well-behaved.

She said to me: "Would you like a biscuit?" She offered to open the tin my mother had brought for her, but I hid behind my mother, afraid to look upon the blotched face with the wild masses of hair that she patted with both hands each time she bent close to speak to anyone.

I remember my mother kept asking her if there was anything she wanted, and she kept replying, "Thank you very much. You are very kind, but there is nothing I want." She got up and did a dance, a kind of *ronggeng* with a sad, tearful smile on her face.

On nights when the moon was full, the cries of the women in the cells could be clearly heard in our house and I heard my mother say that while Ah Suat Ee was generally quiet and well-behaved, sadly dancing the ronggeng for anyone who requested it, on full moon nights she became uncontrollably violent.

Her daughter-in-law, who faithfully visited her every day with a tiffin carrier of food, told us confidentially that on those nights, she would throw herself against the metal bars of the cell, wailing piteously. She would quieten down for a while, her head inclined against the metal bars, its wild masses of hair streaked with grey streaming about her face, her hands gripping the bars. Sometimes, however, she wailed through the night, and the hospital attendant would shout at her for disturbing the peace and threaten to cane her as if she were a child.

With the child's love for stories, I had always gravitated towards any group of adults who appeared to be telling tales or exchanging gossip; often they would shoo me away, but I always managed to linger on the edges of adult conversation, carrying away with me awesome tales of avenging ghosts and blood and death. The wails of demon women crying for their mortal lovers became intermingled with mournful cries from the hospital outhouse on nights of the full moon.

Ah Suat Ee, long before her death, had become a demon woman howling for her lover. The real cause of Ah Suat Ee's mental breakdown had not been love, but money. Having been cheated by an unscrupulous relative of all her life savings which she had put in a tontine, she had lost her mind.

On full moon nights, some men repaired in stealth to graves of women who, like Ah Suat Ee, had died in the violence of dementia, or who, like the mysterious young woman in our neighbourhood whose name I have forgotten, had died giving birth and cursing the faithless father of her child. The spirits of these women were invoked, and requests made for prize-winning numbers in lotteries. In the light of the full moon, these spirits sometimes obliged their human supplicants, sometimes exacting terrible payments for their favours.

As far as I knew, no one had gone to Ah Suat Ee's grave or to the mysterious young woman's grave to ask for numbers. But long after the ravings of these two unhappy women had been stilled in the earth, I heard them, saw them, still in their white death clothes. I pleaded with them but still they would cut off my ear and rebuke me for pointing to the full moon.

The Anniversary

Hong is my aunt's cousin's nephew; we found that out by pure accident when we were studying together at the university.

Finding the relationship too remote to allow for that degree of confidence which he supposed could subsist only between close kin, he simply cut through all the consanguineous convolutions and called himself my cousin. This way, he did not lay himself open to the idle conjectures of fellow undergraduates who saw us together very often – at lectures, in the university canteen, taking evening walks in the campus. The other protection was in our very visible incompatibility, for while I appeared a robust tomboy, Hong was of that species of small-framed, bent and cowed-looking male that must provoke a certain measure of pity.

So, thus doubly defended against the speculations of our friends on the campus. Hong, with all the earnestness of a young man in love, confided in me. He was deeply, hopelessly in love with a girl named Teresa; she had been an undergraduate for only a year, having failed her first-year examinations. A quiet, pretty girl, she had attracted at least half-a-dozen young men in campus, including her tutor, but had shown not the slightest inclination to reciprocate that interest.

Hong persevered to worship her from the long distance imposed both by her coolness and his shyness. Teresa applied to go into the Teachers' Training Institute. It was a two-year programme, which combined coursework and practical training. She spent much time at the library, preparing lesson notes, making teaching aids, and was apparently contented and happy.

All this Hong knew, through whatever secret device he had set up to monitor her movements. He seemed to know exactly what she was doing, when and with whom. He told me one day, with an ecstatic glow on his pale thin face, that he had seen her at a cinema with her sister, and had briefly greeted her. She had smiled in response.

Hong talked about her incessantly in my presence; it had occurred to me long before that he sought no advice, desired no encouragement. All he wanted was a ready listener, and somehow the discovery that I was a cousin of sorts fitted me for that role. He confided that as soon as he had obtained his degree, he would approach her and make clear his feelings. He was very firm on the point that he would make no approach till he had obtained his degree, obviously believing that this would vastly improve his chances.

After graduation, the opportunities to meet lessened as we went our separate ways. Our paths crossed every once in a while, though, and on one occasion he mentioned having met Teresa and that he had reason to be hopeful.

Almost two years elapsed before we met again, and this time it was to announce, with all the fervour and intensity that a habitually shy and reticent man could muster, that Teresa had agreed to marry him. Her grandmother had passed away at about this time, and there would have to be a six-month wait, in compliance with some old custom.

I met them once during the period of their engagement. He had gained weight, and looked much better. There was a new confidence, a new happiness. Whereas Teresa had been merely pretty in a quiet sort of way, she was now glowingly beautiful. It was clear that they were deeply in love. During the lunch, I was constantly aware of being an obtrusive third.

Teresa was to fly to Penang at the end of the six months and perform some rites at her grandmother's grave that would signal the end of the mourning period. There were a whole host of elderly relatives in Penang who would be very pleased by this show of filial piety. Then she would be ready to fly back to Singapore for her wedding, a very quiet and private affair to which they had only invited their closest friends. As the confidante who had patiently listened to Hong during all those years when his timid heart was ready to burst with the secret love it harboured, I felt entitled to be part of that select circle.

I teased the happy couple mercilessly about the letters they were always writing to each other, even when they were separated for only a few days. During the four days when she was in Penang for her grandmother's funeral, Teresa wrote no fewer than six letters, and no doubt received as many.

We did not meet again for some months, although Hong rang me up several times 'just to talk'. His engagement had made no difference to the ready flow of confidential talk; only now it was the happy, accepted lover talking of future plans, not the uncertain restless young man driven by doubts.

I remembered, in a vague sort of way, that Teresa was due to fly home from Penang on the 19th. Therefore when the news of the terrible crash was broadcast in the evening news bulletin, I had an uneasiness which I could not dispel until I had rung Hong up. He was not at home.

Meanwhile, more details about the crash were carried over the radio and television; there were no survivors. The plane had exploded in mid-air and scattered over a radius of several kilometres, in a desolate area of *lallang* and secondary jungle. All the 112 people aboard had been killed.

A few of the people in the neighbouring kampongs had seen the explosion in the sky. There were many theories about the explosion – a bomb planted aboard, a hijack, a suicide attempt by a very important government official fleeing the country. The news made headlines in every newspaper. But the immediate task was to pick up the pieces and identify the dead as far as was possible.

I rang Hong repeatedly, finally someone answered the phone. It was his sister. In a weak voice, she told me that he was under sedation. He had rushed to the airport to find out whether Teresa's name was on the passenger list; it was. Then he made a frantic call to the Penang relatives, and found that one of them had driven Teresa to the airport. There was no hope now. Teresa was among the 112 victims. Hong collapsed, the receiver still tightly in his hand, and had to be helped to the sofa. A doctor was quickly called in. When I saw him then, still reclining on the sofa and weeping unrestrainedly, I realized that the sorrow could not be over easily.

In the days that followed, weakened from lack of food and sleep, he nevertheless rushed around in a frenzy of activity, visiting the site of the terrible tragedy, trying desperately to break through the cordon that the authorities had thrown around the dismal wreckage, to see if he could salvage anything that could even remotely connect him to her. Torsos and limbs were strewn over a wilderness of jungle bushes and grass; they were hurriedly picked up and put in large plastic bags of uniform size. Hong, dishevelled and wild-eyed and supported by his weeping sister and her husband, fell down on his knees in the mud – the operation of cleaning up was going on in spite of heavy rain – and in a paroxysm of bitterness and grief, asked Heaven if it would not even give him a part of Teresa's body to bury in a decent burial, to at least allow him to have something small that he could keep as a remembrance of her.

As if in answer to his prayers, a small suitcase belonging to Teresa was found and put together with the other salvaged belongings – a forlorn heap of burst suitcases, attaché cases, scattered files and letterheads of business organizations, shoes, handbags, even a child's teddy bear.

Hong fell upon it with ferocious possessiveness; the small light-brown suitcase had burst open and was partially scorched, but the name tag was intact.

He went through a pocket on one side of the suitcase and fished out a letter – a long letter written in Teresa's close, neat hand, full of endearments, like the rest of her letters to him. She had written it the day before she left Penang, and had probably decided that it would take a longer time by post than if she were to deliver it herself. Hong broke down on reading the letter; it was her last letter to him, written the day before she was killed.

Hong was at the site every day; what he hoped to do or find, nobody could tell. He hung around, a pathetic picture of grief; he watched every stage of the massive cleaning-up operation, from the gathering of the dismembered parts to be put in large antiseptic plastic bags, to the final laying of these bags in coffins and their internment in a plot of state land amidst prayers offered by a gathering of priests and monks, who formed a complete representation of all the possible faiths of the victims. Hong had asked Father O'Reilly, Teresa's parish priest, to come and offer prayers for her.

As if to work out the tremendous sorrow that was threatening to overpower him, he went about in frenzied activity, offering a mass for her in this church, prayers for the repose of her soul in that church, composing a verse for insertion in the obituary column of *The Straits Times* that would have been maudlin but for the depth of his grief. And still the need to be constantly in motion remained, to put off, as far as possible, that terrible moment of stark awakening to solitude.

The weeks after the crash were the most anxious for Hong's relatives and friends, for it appeared that at any moment, he would slip over the edge. He quietened down, and then all his attention focussed on the precious letter rescued from the wreck. He read it again and again and drew comfort from it, for it was as it his beloved fiancée was speaking words of affection to him from the grave.

He went quietly about his work as a lecturer in the university and occasionally rang me up to talk, sometimes about Teresa, sometimes about inconsequential matters. On the anniversary of her death, he again inserted a message of loving remembrance for her in *The Straits Times*, and had a mass said for her in the church where they used to attend.

It was about a month after the anniversary when Hong suggested having lunch together. All through lunch, he was very subdued and I knew that there was something he wanted to tell me but was hesitant to. He finally brought out a letter from his pocket, that last letter Teresa had written and said, "There's a message in this letter that I should have been alert to; I missed it, and now it's too late."

He made me read the letter, which I did with great discomfort, for here was a very private letter, full of the sentiments of a woman very much in love and wanting, in every word, to give pleasure to the beloved. I hurried through the letter, but there did not seem to be any message of the kind that Hong had hinted at.

"Read it again," said Hong rather impatiently, "read those lines again referring to an anniversary." I skimmed through the letter again; with some difficulty, my eyes picked out, among the mass of closely written lines, this sentence: "Not death will separate us; I shall see you again, dearest, but only on the anniversary."

Isolated, lifted out of context, the sentence had an air of foreboding about it; but as part of a letter almost extravagant in its claims and expressions of love and hope, there was nothing to distinguish it from any of the other sentences.

"Don't you see the significance?" Hong asked. "She had a premonition of death, and there and then decided that death would not separate us. She would return on the anniversary to see me again. But the anniversary's past," he added brokenly. "July 19's past, and I was a fool to have missed the chance. She'll never come again."

"What would you have done?" I asked tentatively, looking at this man still struggling to come to terms with his sorrow.

"I would have gone to the site; she must, have waited for me and I never turned up!" The last words were uttered in an agonized cry of self-reproach.

"Are you sure she was referring to this anniversary? Could she not have meant some other anniversary, for instance, the anniversary of your engagement, your first meeting, your first kiss?" I became frivolous in my anxiety to turn this man away from the dangerous drift of his thoughts.

"Not death will separate us; I shall see you again, dearest, but only on the anniversary," he quoted slowly without looking at the letter. "It could mean nothing else. Don't you see how these words cannot be interpreted in any other way? Fool! Fool that I am for missing this message for a whole year." Again he berated himself for his gross negligence, and this time he pounded the side of his head with a clenched fist.

"I must go," he said fiercely. "I must go to the site and find out whether she's been there. There are some Malay kampongs around. Somebody would have seen."

"Let me go with you," I ventured, "or get your sister to go with you." Then, fearing he would regard this as offensive patronage by the wise of the weak-minded, I quickly added, "I would like to, really."

The site was inaccessible by car; we walked for some distance through overgrown grass and lallang, and I saw that Hong was weeping silently. Here and there were desolate reminders of the tragedy: a small part of the plane now rusting and covered with coarse grass, an object partly submerged in the ground that must have been a plane seat, for the remnants of a seat-belt were still attached to it.

Hong and I looked around for a while, then walked for some distance towards a small cluster of Malay huts on the edge. In halting Malay, Hong asked questions to find out if the little band of curious onlookers who had gathered in front of us could remember the plane crash. They nodded their heads vigorously. One of them, an old man with brown stumps for teeth, said that he had witnessed the explosion in the sky. He made a loud sound and lifted both arms to convey the force of the explosion.

One of the young men cried out shrilly, "*Ada hantu! Ada hantu!*" and pointed to the site of the crash, while the women showed signs of fear. One of them gestured to him to stop talking.

Hong's voice quavered in excitement as he persuaded and then threatened the young man to talk further. But the young man, in response to the woman's warning, suddenly became tight-lipped. They seemed to realize that they were on the edge of something incomprehensible and dangerous and must withdraw. But there was no stopping Hong. Tearfully, he offered money. The group slunk away sullenly, but the old man with the rotting teeth, sensing the urgency in Hong's voice, returned to tell him what they had seen.

About a month before, late in the evening, they had heard cries from the site of the accident – human voices, not the cries of lonely owls or other night creatures of the jungle. The cries gradually became louder: women's voices shrieking, a child's wail. The old man had actually walked out to see what was happening; he ran back when he saw figures moving about the waste ground, shadowy figures moving about in great urgency. There was no plane, only a massing together of dark human shapes who appeared to have lost their way.

"*Hantu, hantu,*" cried the old man, shaking his head slowly. The *hantu* of all those who had died in the crash. How else could you explain the large number, the plaintive cries?

"She was there, as she had promised," sobbed Hong as we made our way back. "About a month ago, the old Malay man said. That was the anniversary, don't you see? And I have missed it. I don't know whether she'll come for the next anniversary."

I was too bewildered to do anything except repeatedly nod assent; this easily perceived and reassuring form relieved me of all necessity of following Hong's tortured train of thoughts as we drove back, so that I could sort things out in my own mind.

The sequel to this story is most depressing. Hong suffered a nervous breakdown and was temporarily relieved of his duties at the university. He stays at home, obsessed by the pain of having missed the only chance of granting the last affectionate request of a deeply-loved woman, and waits impatiently for the next anniversary to come. He says she appeared to him in a dream and reproached him for not keeping the appointment. She said that she had waited a very long time for him to come, and asked why he never did.

Hong's appearance has all the signs of a man no longer in control of himself. His hair has grown long; he is unshaven and unkempt, his clothes unwashed. He waits for July 19; and only the thought of July 19 keeps him alive.

"I shall be quite happy to die after that," he says simply. "I shall wait for the anniversary for her to come again and then I shall see what she wants me to do. I should be quite happy to die after that, you know."

The Exhumation

The notice of exhumation of graves was gazetted in *The Straits Times*; it was one of a rapid series of exhumation notices, for the government was impatient to reclaim the land from the dead to build houses and offices and supermarkets for the living.

Before the bulldozers moved in, there was a flurry of activity on the part of my relatives, for grandmother's grave was one of those in the marked cemetery, and everybody wanted to be assured that the old lady, who had lain in the earth these 30 years, would not be unduly upset by the disturbance.

The first of the pacification rites was held at home, in front of the ancestral altar, over which hung a large portrait of grandmother.

As a child, I had once observed a similar rite in which a member of the family expressed his contrition to a deceased relative – I cannot recollect what the offence was – but I remember the family member clasping a handful of lit joss-sticks and moving them up and down in front of the portrait, and repeatedly striking his chest in penitential sorrow. This time, I watched with much interest the efforts at pacifying the spirit of my grandmother.

Joss-sticks were burnt and prayers chanted, but I took no part in the ceremony, believing it would conflict with my Christian beliefs. So I watched, an interested, curious and sometimes amused observer, especially when one of my aunts, a very old lady of 70, began talking to grandmother in the casual way she must have done when grandmother was alive.

Aunt, looking up at grandmother's portrait, and clasping a joss-stick in her hands, delivered a severe tirade on grandmother's behalf against a merciless government that would plunder the homes of the dead. The speech, interrupted by the loud raucous sounds of the clearing of phlegm from the throat, all the more resembled a natural conversation, and it was hard not to picture grandmother listening and nodding in vigorous agreement. Several times Aunt asked for forgiveness, presumably for the government of Singapore.

Grandmother, represented by the framed photograph above the ancestral altar with its comfortably familiar joss-sticks, scented flowers and oranges, was not in the least frightening. But grandmother, underneath the huge slat) of grey marble bearing her name, date of birth and date of death, did cause a shiver or two.

I stood with the others surveying her tombstone, surrounded by tall lallang despite the fact that only six months before, the grass had been trimmed in preparation for the Feast of the Hungry Ghosts.

I had insisted on coming, impelled more by curiosity and by that combination of adventurousness and frivolity that belonged to that period of life.

I watched further pacification ceremonies; this time, a priest was called to say prayers over the grave in preparation for the actual ceremony of exhumation. My relatives would not hear of the impersonal business-like mass exhumation provided by the government for only a small charge; a private ceremony was preferable, though much more costly.

I have almost come to believe that those people who make their living by close contact with the dead, such as morticians and embalmers, resemble the dead. The stereotype of the tall, pale embalmer with the huge sunken eyes, hollow cheeks and sepulchral stare is, I am now almost persuaded, based on truth, for all the embalmers and exhumers I have seen look like this or get to look like this, as if in concession to their calling.

The exhumers for grandmother's grave – there were two of them – looked just like resurrected corpses: two old, ashen-skinned men, stripped to the waist for the messy work of prodding about in the soggy ground around a rotting coffin ready to surrender its contents, moving about mechanically with expressionless faces, and now and again looking up with glazed eyes. Awed respectfulness was owing to the dead only if they were remote enough. Here, touching and picking up bones, the exhumers had no need of it.

The coffin was too deeply embedded in waterlogged earth to be heaved up, and the two exhumers had to prise open the coffin lid, which they managed to very easily and expertly.

Peering down, I caught a glimpse of a heap of bones, with only the skull distinguishable, covered in muddy water.

I looked away – for it was the most desolate sight in the world, and I was overcome by a crushing sense of mortality. I had seen death, but somehow this heap of waterlogged bones that had been my grandmother, whom I remembered as a robust, severe-looking woman who bought bondmaids to be trained to work for her in her bridal furnishing business, troubled and saddened me beyond words.

In the distance, in a cemetery that had just been cleared, the relentless sound of piling had already begun. Grandmother's remains were quickly removed and taken away by the exhumers to be cleaned properly before they were consigned to the crematorium. Grandmother's ashes would then be stored in a stone casket and laid to rest finally in a niche in a government columbarium.

Throughout the exhumation ceremony, we had our

handkerchiefs to our noses. By some strange twist of logic, I had persuaded myself that this was a mark of great discourtesy to a dead ancestor, and had been prepared to brave any discomfort rather than resort to my handkerchief. But when I saw everybody else nonchalantly covering up their noses, I did the same – with relief, for the odour was unbearable. Wasn't it odd, I thought, for the flesh had long since gone, but perhaps the earth around it had been imbibed with centuries of decay which was surrendered readily, once disturbed.

That night we had dreams of grandmother – all of us. Some of the dreams were inconsequential, but I, who knew grandmother only from the dreadful stories I had heard about her severity towards the bondmaids and towards grandfather, and also from the one or two visits I had made to her house when I was a child, had the most vivid dream of all.

In my dream, grandmother was present at her own exhumation. She took me by the hand and led me to a grassy verge from which a small group of people were watching the two exhumers at work.

We stood there together and I was all the while conscious of a puzzling thought. How could grandmother be standing there with me, holding my hand when she had been dead these 30 years? For sometimes reality intrudes into dreams in the most devastating way.

I looked up at her face, and it was a corpse's face; when it slowly turned to look upon me, I was aware of an overpowering sensation of horror though I did not try to break away. Her grip upon my arm tightened and finally I burst out with the words, "Please, grandmother, don't do this to me!"

I woke up at this point and did not dare go back to sleep, fearful that the dream might return. I woke the family up and related the dream to them. They too had dreamt of grandmother.

They listened intently to my narration, and then the aunt who had conversed with grandmother at the altar took hold of my arm, looked closely at it and exclaimed that grandmother had left the imprint of her fingers on my flesh. I recoiled, protesting; there were indeed some faint imprints on my arm, but they were not the imprints of fingers, probably the impression of the ribbed pattern of a pillow or blanket pressed closed in sleep.

Aunt had dreamt of grandmother too: grandmother was on her death-bed, with tears running silently down the sides of her face on to her pillow. This aunt interpreted to mean that grandmother's spirit was distressed at the disturbance of her grave.

How could it be explained, except by the presence of a dead rat in the house or a dead cat outside whose odour the wind wafted in through the window at the time of our talking about grandmother? But we were, all at once, aware of a powerful smell.

I had heard of people smelling jasmine at the precise moment of the death of a loved one, but this smell was frightful. It lasted more than two or three minutes, during which we shifted and sniffed uncomfortably.

Someone whispered, “She’s here,” and then broke into the same chant of propitiation that had been uttered days before in front of the altar.

Of Blood From Woman

"May she vomit blood on her death-bed, and may she then die!"

The curse, rendered in English, loses a great deal of its alarming vehemence; there probably are not words enough in the English language to convey the sheer force of Chinese vituperations. It is the totality of facial expression, the physical act of dragging the words out, as of a monstrous birth, and above all, of the whole force of tradition going back to countless generations, that invests each image with a power and a terror that cannot be explained by meaning alone.

"May she vomit blood on her death-bed, and may she then die!"

I remember the utterance, made amidst great convulsive sobs by a young woman against an elderly woman who had done everything in her power to thwart her husband's taking in this young woman as his second wife. The weeping woman was standing in front of an ancestral altar; by thus inviting the spirits to bear witness, she had put the stamp of irrevocability on the curse.

Sometimes, for the same purpose, a curse was uttered in the presence of thunder and lightning. The picture of a dying man or woman spewing blood – that was one of the most terrifying images of my childhood.

I once heard of a coffin that somehow slipped the grasp of the pallbearers so that it crashed to the ground, burst open and threw out the corpse, a very fat old woman. And I had read somewhere of a degenerate English king whose deceased, bloated corpse had to be squeezed into the coffin which actually burst open in the church itself, flooding the church floor with blood.

All these images had fused in my fervid imagination into a scene of the most frightful kind, and for a long time blood became associated with all that was sinister and direful.

I had an aunt who had attended, though never participated, in seances with the dead at gravesides. The purpose of calling up the dead was often to seek their help in getting the winning numbers of lotteries. Aunt was an inveterate gambler and claimed that she had won on several occasions with the numbers given by the spirits.

What did they look like? Very often you could not see them distinctly, said Aunt. Once she saw a faint colour of smoke, and another time, she felt a strange indescribable chill overcome her and heard a kind of rasping voice.

How were the spirits called up? What had to be done first? Blood, said Aunt. The blood of a white cockerel freshly slaughtered at the graveside. This was absolutely indispensable. The blood was then poured through a hollow bamboo stick stuck near the grave, certain prayers were chanted and the spirit would then rise.

Blood to make a man die, blood to bring him money – and blood to make him a good husband. For blood from woman was the most potent, it was claimed, to make a man love you and treat you well.

I had often been fascinated by this method of securing a man's love; a woman, desperate for the charm to work, actually made use of each monthly emission. The blood was mixed in food which was then offered to the unsuspecting object of desire. The charm was said to be the most potent of all the charms to win the total love of a husband or lover.

I remember that there was a half-Thai woman who lived in the town for a while; an old, fat, gross-looking woman whose mouth and teeth were a permanent bright red from the betel nut and sireh she was always chewing. She had had three husbands; her fourth was 13 years younger – a handsome, quiet and refined fellow who had a good job in some government department and who never looked at another woman. The half-Thai woman, complacent in this man's total love and devotion, made no secret of the means by which this subjection to her will had been secured, and actually taught other women how to go about achieving the same happiness.

As a girl, I could not see beyond the bizarre element of this charm; it was only later that I saw its terrifying symbolism. Woman, who had always been held as inferior and was expected to be subject to her menfolk – her father, her brothers and later her husband – and who during her menstrual period was regarded as so unclean that any major disaster was attributed to her failure to stay away during this period of uncleanliness, was now having her revenge. She was having a secret and malicious chuckle against men who wanted her body but blamed it for misfortunes that happened to them. Fishermen would never allow a woman near if they wanted a successful expedition; timber-loggers venturing into the vast wilds where spirits dwelt in every tree, would never permit the contaminating presence of a woman.

And now, said the woman with a secret glee, you who would have my body but condemn it as unclean, drink this or eat this! The half-Thai woman embodied, in the most revolting way, this dark triumph of woman. She spoke in a rough, raucous voice to her husband, demanded his full pay packet and if he so much as looked at another woman, berated him soundly and hurled obscenities at him. He took it all meekly; people shook their heads knowingly and spoke of the secret source of the woman's power.

Perhaps only once in her life was blood of woman not considered evil, but actually good and even capable of driving away harmful spirits. Hymeneal blood, ultimate proof of chastity on her marriage bed, and captured on a clean white piece of linen, was reverently stored and put away, its presence thereby repelling evil and attracting prosperity for her husband and harmony for the household.

Lee Geok Chan

Lee Geok Chan was one of my students in pre-university. One of the many for whom long hours of study ensured, at most, a scraping through the examinations. She was a pale, small-sized, earnest-looking girl, always seen with a book or a sheaf of notes in her hand. Her father was a tailor, her mother a washerwoman; there were three brothers and two sisters. Geok Chan was the second in the family and the eldest girl.

Her desire to pass the examination, get a job and help the family put her in a constant state of nervous effort, so that she was to be found at all times blinking anxiously as she took down a teacher's lecture verbatim, copying notes from the blackboard with extreme diligence, or writing an essay with a concentration all the more remarkable for the noise and complete abandon of those around her in the classroom.

I always found it painful to have to tell Geok Chan, in response to her timid inquiry of how she could improve in her written expression, that her English was rather weak, her use of words frequently inappropriate, and that she often strayed off the point in her essay. She would nod in docile agreement, but at the same time the disappointment showed visibly on her face. Additional lessons did not seem to have helped and each week it became a special pain for me to hand back a piece of work, to see it snatched up eagerly and checked for its grade, and then to see the crestfallen look on the thin, pale face.

Like so many others, Geok Chan was preparing for the A-level examinations at the end of the year. In the last month before the examination, she often came up to me with a quick nervous smile and handed me a sheaf of essays to mark.

One of the essays caught my attention. It was better than the others; in fact, it was the best she had ever written, and there was hope yet, for her, if she could produce something like that in the examination. I forget the exact words of the essay topic she had picked from somewhere, but it was about happiness. Geok Chan had written simply and with conviction about her concept of happiness; some parts of the essay were, I thought, beautifully lyrical. I suddenly realized that, freed from the constraints of conventional essay topics, she wrote with ease and obvious pleasure.

I called her up and commented favourably on her essay. She glowed with pride. "If I write like that in the General Paper, will I get a credit?" she wanted to know. I had to warn her, rather sadly, that the essay topics in the General Paper were not of the kind that permitted this spontaneity. I encouraged her, though, to go on expressing her innermost feelings.

"They're in me all the time. I couldn't express them before, now I think I can," she said, blinking not with nervousness but, instead, with a kind of feverish joy.

On the morning of the essay paper, Geok Chan was killed in a road accident. She was walking along the pavement just outside the school and was about to enter the school gates when a lorry came racing along, crazily jumped the road divider and crashed into her. She died instantly. It was the most cruel death I had ever known; my colleagues and I wept long for this earnest, good girl who had always tried her best and whose only ambition was to earn enough to support her family.

The essay on happiness that had astonished me by its power and lyricism lay, among a pile of unmarked papers on my desk, almost like a keepsake, for she had collected all the other essays, and had somehow left this one with me. When I went to see her parents, who were too grieved to say anything, I brought this composition with me and handed it to her eldest brother, who just put it aside with her other school things heaped on a little wooden table in the small two-room HDB flat.

The recollection of that small body under sheets of newspapers on the road disturbed me for many days afterwards. The blood had flowed copiously; it was a moment's glance before I turned away and quickly walked back to the staff room from where we had been summoned by the frantic cries of those students who had witnessed the dreadful accident. But the scene stayed in my mind for days, and it was inevitable that some of us would have had dreams about Lee Geok Chan in our sleep.

I dreamt that she approached me with a poem on sorrow or something like that and asked me to grade it. Another colleague dreamt of her exactly as she was that day, under the newspapers on a wet road just in front of the school gate.

In the bustle of a new school year when new eager faces crowded the school corridors, Lee Geok Chan was soon forgotten. Occasionally, however, something or other cropped up to remind us of her and then we recollected that terrible day in December.

One occasion was the release of the examination results in March. Students started coming to the school very early in the morning, as soon as they had learnt from the newspaper that the Ministry of Education would be releasing the results that day. The computer print-out with Geok Chan's name showed the grades for these subjects – History, Chinese Language and the General Paper. She had obtained a credit in Chinese Language, but had failed for History and the General Paper.

There had to be a mistake regarding the General Paper – how could there have been a grade for that subject? Geok Chan was killed before she could sit for the paper. Her death was in the morning; the paper was at two in the afternoon.

It was a very low grade, in fact the lowest on the scale. If a computer had to make a mistake about one who was already dead, some of us laughed uneasily, surely it could have erred on the side of generosity?

Geok Chan's elder brother came to collect the results slip, which he did desultorily, without a glance at the statements on the slip, and was gone almost immediately.

I first of all ascertained from the Minister of Education that there had been no mistake in the print-out; then I wrote a very polite letter to the Cambridge Syndicate of Examiners, asking them to explain why the essay of the candidate Lee Geok Chan had obtained such a low grade. It was a laborious process involving excessive red tape, for there were certain formalities to be gone through, including the payment of a stipulated sum of money.

It took Cambridge a month to reply. I received a plain official statement on how the candidate had gone entirely out of point in the essay section, for she had written a piece on happiness when there was no essay topic even remotely resembling this. The statement added that by itself the essay was commendable for its expressiveness and strength of feeling, but since it was written in total disregard of the given examination topics, it could not be awarded any marks.

The mounting sensation of excitement and terror that gripped me as I read the statement was something I had never experienced before. It was impossible to contain the thoughts that were now crowding my mind, and I soon found myself in urgent consultation with my colleagues. It cannot be, it cannot be, we said again and again. And yet again and again, no matter how hard we tried, no matter how many theories we tested, there was no accounting for the fact that the essay which had been sent to Cambridge together with thousands of other essays, and which had been marked and given a grade, was the essay of a dead student.

Unable to let things lie, I wrote to Cambridge again and requested, urgently, to have the essay script of candidate Lee Geok Chan returned. I added that I was prepared to pay any amount of money that the authorities might deem reasonable to compensate them for their pains.

Probably fearing that a move of this kind could set the precedent for anxious parents or teachers intending to fine-toothcomb a marked script and argue for a better grade, the Cambridge Syndicate turned down the request. It had never been and would never be their policy to return marked scripts to candidates. All they were prepared to do was furnish a statement about the script, and they had already done this.

But this is no ordinary script, a dead person wrote it, I wanted to cry out in exasperation when I read the reply. Then I realized how nearly impossible it would be to give this explanation in the circumscribed language of formal correspondence. I tried, though, so eager was I to get to the bottom of it all, but after a while Cambridge chose not to reply to my requests, probably dismissing me as a crank.

I almost pleaded with them to send me a typewritten copy of the candidate's essay, so that the marking and grading of the script could remain confidential, but they must have misinterpreted the tone of the letter and taken offence, for they finally wrote back to say that they would no longer entertain any correspondence on the subject.

I tried to enlist the help of Geok Chan's family, but it was to no avail. The elder brother had been posted to some other town; the younger brothers and sisters did not seem able to understand me and the parents spoke only a dialect I could not comprehend. In any case, they were still too sorrowful to do much beyond shaking their heads mournfully or raising their voices to curse the driver of the lorry that had killed their daughter.

It is now more than 10 years since Lee Geok Chan died. I am not satisfied with the explanation that my colleagues finally settled on. A coincidence, they said, somebody's essay was mistaken for Geok Chan's; after all, there were thousands of essays to be graded and confusions of this kind were not at all surprising.

But the topic was so specific. It was on happiness, I protested, the very same topic she wrote on just before the accident. And the qualities of freshness and expressiveness were precisely those I had noted in that last essay she showed me. That could not have been a coincidence; there must have been a mistake then, said some of my colleagues. A coincidence, a mistake – the words threw a blanket over all that remains, to this day, a mystery.

Two Male Children

The house bulged with people. If there were too many people, it was not the consequence of want but choice, for the patriarch had insisted that all the married sons continue to stay in the family house while married daughters could leave if they so wished.

He had grown up in China, where married sons and their families stayed with the parents. But whereas over there a certain amount of privacy was afforded by the separating courtyards, here the families piled into the rooms of two adjoining double-storeyed shophouses, the dividing wall of which had been torn down to form one continuous unit.

The old patriarch was very rich, for he had invested shrewdly in coconut and rubber plantations and owned row upon row of shophouses in town. But he had fixed ideas about how money was to be spent, and comfortable living conditions were not one of them. At a time when much less affluent families were buying Dunlopillo mattresses and pillows, refrigerators and even Ford cars, he was still sleeping on cotton-stuffed mattresses and the women in his household were depending solely on wooden food-cupboards with wire-netting doors and legs standing in thick earthen bowls filled with water to prevent the ants from getting at the cooked food kept in the cupboards.

As for cars, he clearly had no intention of owning any or allowing his three sons who were helping him in his business to own any. He was sole proprietor of a fleet of buses which brought him a very good income, and he gave his relatives, who numbered hundreds, free bus passes.

The patriarch was by no means niggardly; in matters concerning male progeny he could be astonishingly extravagant. His three sons produced no male children; every year saw a new granddaughter or two and the old man was heard to snort in disgust each time he received news of yet one more granddaughter. He had given his wife thousands of dollars to spend on prayers, good deeds, ceremonial offerings and so on, recommended by temple priests and mediums for the begetting of a grandson. But the money had been futilely spent, and in the end, the old man resigned himself to the prospect of a very long wait for a grandson.

His remark that the biggest share of the property would go to the first grandson was construed as a warning by the three sons and had immediately set in motion an almost frenzied contest among the three daughters-in-law to see who would be the first to produce the male heir. At any one time, one of the three would be pregnant, but the fecundity was all in the direction of female offspring. There was much hidden animosity among the three women, though they shared the work harmoniously enough in the huge smoky kitchen.

Two servants were employed to help take care of the younger grandchildren. One of them was a friendly, big-hearted woman who dropped in at our house quite frequently for a chat. She always came with a child on her hips, and sometimes a bowl of the child's porridge. And while feeding the child, she would chat amiably with the womenfolk, who were always eager for tidbits of gossip from the Great House.

This servant, whose name was Ah Chan, had two sons and must have been the envy of the three daughters-in-law. She was now pregnant a third time, and so was the First Daughter-in-law who, after three daughters, felt sure her fourth would be a boy. Her mother had gone to consult a fortune-teller who had told her that this time it would be a son.

Both Ah Chan and First Daughter-in-law gave birth to sons. While Ah Chan grieved that she still had to wait for a daughter, everyone in the Great House was full of excitement at the birth of the long-awaited first grandson. The old man was jubilant and his wife equally so. The two other daughters-in-law, chagrined that the prize was now lost to them, had to content themselves firstly with the wish that they, too, in the appointed time, would have male children, and secondly, with the observation made only to each other, that the new-born baby was a sickly, puny little thing, quite unlike Ah Chan's healthy baby son.

The new grandchild, whose name was deliberated on by at least three fortune-tellers, gave cause for much anxiety for he cried often, drank poorly and did not seem to put on any weight. His mother cried in her anxiety and fretted that she did not produce enough milk for the infant.

To her, it was the height of injustice that her baby, heir to the rubber and coconut plantations, should be sickly and underfed, while Ah Chan's baby, one of the hundreds born in her kampong every year and who would probably grow up to be a mean labourer, was robust from his mother's brimming good health.

The new grandson, eventually given the name 'Golden Dragon', pulled through the first month. There was great, rejoicing. Every family in the neighbourhood received the celebratory yellow rice, red-stained hard-boiled eggs and red-stained bean-cakes.

The baby boy was brought downstairs for the first time that day, a frail thing decked out in pink clothes, pink woollen cap and pink bootees. The baby's thin fingers and ankles glistened with gold ornaments, presents from numerous relatives.

Ah Chan's son, who had been affectionately nicknamed 'Piglet' by her family, had cleared his first month a few days before, but there was no expensive celebration. By the fourth month, Piglet was almost twice the size of Golden Dragon, a fact that the other two sisters-in-law were heard to observe more than once, and twice as rapid in his development, for he could turn over on his side, recognize his parents and smile and gurgle in response to his brothers.

Golden Dragon continued to be sickly, and in his fifth month was suddenly taken ill. It seemed to be a bad time for infants; Piglet was unwell too, and Ah Chan, who had grown very attached to this third son although she had badly wanted a daughter, rushed home from the Great House every evening to look after him.

Golden Dragon's condition worsened visibly; his parents and grandparents flew into a panic and immediately went to consult a temple medium. On the first visit, they secured an amulet which they placed against the baby's chest. The baby's condition did not improve. On the second visit, they were told by the temple medium who had gone into a trance that the "Dark Deity of Hell" wanted a boy attendant, had searched for one and had taken a fancy to Golden Dragon. Golden Dragon would die soon.

A flurry of consultations with temple mediums ensued; thousands of dollars were spent in gifts of propitiation and entreaty to the Dark Deity of Hell, but still he would, according to the temple mediums, have Golden Dragon. However, said one of the temple mediums from his deep trance, the Dark Deity was also considering one other male child, who was born at about the same time and who was also now lying ill. If one of the baby boys died, the other would be spared.

Here was hope yet, and the grandmother and mother began to fill the baby's room with all manner of charms and amulets to ward off evil influence and deflect it elsewhere. Ah Chan came to know of the message from the temple medium but by that time, it had been distorted into an accusation. The Dark Deity of Hell had chosen Piglet to be his boy attendant but Piglet deflected the curse which then fell on Golden Dragon.

Ah Chan, in her simplicity, went tremblingly to her employers in the Great House to beg for forgiveness. The grandmother and the mother of Golden Dragon received her coldly. They were now convinced of the treachery of Piglet, for his mother was now frankly admitting it and asking for forgiveness on his behalf. The act of reparation was simple, according to the temple mediums. Ah Chan's milk would help restore the infant to health.

Ah Chan was only too grateful for this opportunity to make amends; she came early in the morning, leaving only late at night when she returned to feed her own son. During the day, a relative sometimes brought him to the Great House to be fed by his mother. But the illness had had a toll on him, and he was no longer the chubby, rosy baby he once was.

Seeing that their baby was improving, although slightly, the grandmother and relative paid another visit to the temple medium to seek his advice about how to expedite his recovery. The temple medium said that the infant's 'milk mother' had to remain with him day and night.

Ah Chan was thereafter enjoined to stay in the Great House and not to go home. "But what about my baby?" she faltered, for her baby was indeed fretting for her.

Her baby was brought in during the day; at night, it was no longer possible to do the same, and while Golden Dragon drew nourishment from Ah Chan's robust body, Piglet declined for the want of it.

"Please let me go back to my baby," she pleaded, but Golden Dragon's mother promised to send someone to bring him, and his grandmother pressed a gift of money into her hands.

There was the suggestion that Piglet be brought to stay in the Great House with his mother, but the grandmother would not hear of it because the temple medium had said the two babies must not live under the same roof. One would be the means of harm befalling the other. This meant that Piglet could not be brought to the Great House during the day.

By then, the harassed Ah Chan had entrusted a relative with the care of Piglet, to make sure that he was given his powdered milk regularly throughout the day, but this relative was a dull-witted woman who moved about clumsily and slothfully.

One night, at about midnight, she went to the Great House, knocked on the door and shouted for Ah Chan. Her baby was very ill. Ah Chan rushed back, but it was already too late.

The cause of death was later found to be this: the senseless woman had been using an unwashed spoon to stir Piglet's milk, the same spoon that she had been using to take her medicine for a throat infection. The baby had caught the infection, fretted for two days without anybody suspecting anything, and finally succumbed.

Ah Chan could not be comforted; she wept for many days, and moaned the sad fate of an infant identified by the implacable Dark Deity of Hell.

The grandmother hastened over when she heard of the death of Piglet, and pressed yet more money into Ah Chan's hands.

Back in the Great House, Golden Dragon's mother looked at her baby peacefully asleep in its cradle, its cheeks beginning to round up with flesh, and rejoiced that she need fear the Dark Deity no more.

A Soldier Stalks

The places that were assigned us were supposed to be the ideal setting for our work of producing innovative materials for schoolchildren – old quaint colonial-type houses in a sprawling campus setting of lush greenery, including very old and rare trees. There were the friendly, stiff-tailed squirrels in the trees which sometimes ran along the sides of the windows or across our paths; the birds that built nests in the bushes near the outhouses at the back of each building, the occasional vivid-green chameleons that darted across the road and into the roadside bushes before you could draw attention to them.

The ideal bucolic setting for the writer, in need of constant inspiration to bring out his creativity; away from the austere formality of the Ministry Headquarters! Only we, ingrates that we were, persisted in seeing the peeling paint of the walls, the creaking wooden floors of the upstairs rooms, the encrustations of dirt in the bathroom that no amount of scrubbing could hope to remove.

A short time, however, was sufficient to grumble

away these annoyances, and then we found ourselves beginning to look around and quite ready to be worked upon by the charming rusticity of our new-environment.

There was an additional charm: the place had been used by Japanese soldiers during the Occupation, and was said to be full of underground tunnels, all linked together to form a remarkable subterranean backdrop for adventure. Would these tunnels, if we could find them and venture into them, yield skulls and bones? Or hoards of treasure hidden by the Japanese who never managed to secrete them out of the country?

The intoxication was brief; we soon became too preoccupied with work to give much thought to the tunnels, and except for a story about children discovering a trunk of gold bars in a secret crypt, they were soon forgotten.

Somebody had said that the houses were haunted; every house, apparently, had been the scene of a suicide, every old tree outside had had a ghost hanging from it. It became a favourite diversion of the more waggish among us to make frightening noises, rap on doors and windows, especially in the gathering dusk, for there were always a few who never went home before seven, when darkness had already settled and wrapped everything in gloom.

For a time, I joined the small intrepid band whose preference was to stay back and work till dinner than not meet a deadline. It was an unusually dark day. As was my habit, I sat at the typewriter and waited patiently when the lights went off, as they did a few times a day, usually coming on again after a few minutes.

In the darkness I thought I heard somebody cough; it sounded very near and I gave a start, but when the lights came on again and I saw no one, I concluded it must have been one of the security guards outside making his usual rounds.

The footsteps of one of the guards on the gravel outside the window were actually reassuring. I continued with my typing, and once again, to my great annoyance, the lights failed. Making a mental note to complain about this to the Administration the next morning, I leaned back in my chair and decided, when the lights came on again, to pack up and go home.

The lights did not come on for a full five minutes. I sat very still in my chair. I distinctly heard heavy breathing near me; indeed, so near, I could feel it on my shoulder.

I got up quickly, gathered up my handbag and umbrella, and strode quickly to the door. Remembering that I had not turned off the light switches and that I could not risk having the lights on for the whole night, I turned back quickly.

As I groped to turn off the switch, I felt something lightly brushing my face. It felt like or it could have been fingers, or a large butterfly, but at this point I could not hold back my terror any more. I tore down the stairs, my heels making such a tremendous clatter on the wooden stairs that one of the security guards out on the road must have heard me. He came quickly, torch in hand, to ask what was the matter. I merely shook my head, not wanting to stop to talk to anyone, and fled.

This was the beginning of a week of strange happenings, involving several people besides myself. Somehow, I did not relate these experiences to my colleagues the next morning; I did not want to appear foolish and above all, I did not care to hear those oft-heard explanations of overwork and overwrought nerves. I was convinced that there was something unusual and that I had not imagined anything. The cough, the heavy breathing, the light brush of fingers – I could not have imagined them all. When one of my colleagues decided to stay back to finish her work, I, most unaccountably, offered to stay back with her. Perhaps I desperately needed confirmation of my experience; perhaps the presence of another person would take away the terror, would even add piquancy to the experience.

We both settled down to work at our desks after making ourselves hot drinks; our desks were on opposite sides of the room. Rose, a very hard-working person who, once she settled clown to work, unconsciously adopted an austere mien that repulsed every attempt at idle chat, wrote for a while, then looked up.

"Did you cough? I seem to be hearing a cough." I did hear it, and only waited to see if Rose had heard it as well.

"It sounds like a man coughing," I said. We both sat up and listened. The cough seemed to be getting fainter, and then it disappeared.

"Strange," said Rose, frowning, and then almost immediately, we heard the sound of footsteps outside our room – the heavy sounds of hobnailed boots.

We waited for the sounds to die away before we decided to leave. "Very odd," said Rose again, and as we were descending the stairs, she suddenly screamed.

"Somebody touched my face!" she gasped. Somebody had touched me too; I could feel something like a wet pad slapping across my mouth.

I told Rose of my experiences the night before, and we decided not to mention the strange happenings to anyone, sensing that little good would come from the disclosure. Supposing that I had imagined the happenings that night when I was alone, and that I had telepathically communicated my fears to Rose so that she was hearing the same cough, feeling the same ghostly touch? As long as this was a possibility, we felt we could not make known these strange happenings to our colleagues, the more timid of whom were sure to be petrified.

But there was no need for secrecy; soon we found ourselves talking freely about our experiences, because it suddenly seemed as if almost everyone had, in the last few days, heard or felt the presence of this being. A recurring detail in the descriptions was the cough – a hollow, tubercular kind of cough – and then the sound of boots, and the touch of fingers.

Nobody ever saw him; nevertheless all were convinced he was a soldier. Many Japanese soldiers, it was said, preferred suicide to the ignominy of surrender.

Nobody dared stay till dark any more; as soon as the shadows gathered in the trees, we left. One of the security guards claimed to have seen, in the dim light of the moon, a man under a tree near one of the houses. The silhouette showing peaked cap and gun was decidedly that of a soldier. When the guard went near with his torch, there was nobody there. The guard's subsequent illness (which could be attributed as much to his heavy intake of toddy as to having encountered a ghost) further contributed to the tense atmosphere that now pervaded.

Ghosts were no longer a joking matter; the ghost of a soldier stalked the campus, and had been heard and seen by several people. The last person to be affected by all the nervousness was Teng, the artist who produced all the superb illustrations for our children's stories. Unperturbed by the mounting tension that was spreading in widening circles in the campus, he went about his work, sometimes staying as late as nine. He listened to the stories of the strange presence in a half-amused, half-mocking manner.

One morning, his colleague found him slumped over his desk in a state of seeming exhaustion; he had apparently been working with extraordinary intensity at a piece of artwork which now lay under his right hand, the drawing pencil still between his fingers. He was helped up, and the paper gently removed; it showed the face of a soldier, with high cheek-bones and small eyes.

It was some time before Teng could speak coherently of what had happened. He said he was doing his work when something – or someone – seemed to overcome him – he kept describing it as a kind of 'weight' or 'force' which settled on him, so that he could hardly breathe. When shown the picture of the soldier, Teng swore he did not draw it, or was at least not aware that he had drawn it.

For a while, the mysterious picture of the soldier became the focus of much nervous curiosity or pure terror; nobody dared remove it from Teng's desk. Teng's colleagues watched with apprehensiveness the artist's increasingly bizarre behaviour – he was often muttering to himself, sometimes laughing out loud for no apparent reason. Once when he came to see me in connection with some illustrations for stories, there was a frighteningly vacant look in his eyes. Then, one morning, screaming obscenities, he set fire to the picture of the soldier. There was then no choice but to send him home for a long period of rest and medical attention.

That was almost a year ago. After the spate of strange events, culminating in Teng's wild destruction of the picture, things quietened down. No other encounters were reported. There had been talk of getting a priest or monk to cleanse the place and lay the ghost; somehow, the weeks went by and nothing was done. As the happenings ceased and the terror subsided, it was assumed that there was nothing more to fear.

Sometimes, I suddenly pause in the middle of my work because I think there is someone behind me; I turn and invariably there is no one. Many of my colleagues get this sudden strange sensation of someone standing behind their chair. Rose never stays in the room alone, not even during the day; she is continually looking up from her work to ascertain that there is at least one colleague nearby, and sometimes when she bustles about and chats with nervous energy, I know it is because she wants to distract herself from the disturbing recollection of the soldier that stalks the campus.

"I wish I had never seen that picture," she says, closing her eyes with a pained expression. "I can't seem to get it off my mind." Rose talks vaguely about a transfer back to school or to Headquarters. "I don't suppose he'll pursue me there," she says.

I wish I could throw a romantic aura over this lonely, intense man who has been walking the earth these 40 years, consign him to the misty world of ethereal beings that mystifies, even charms. But the soldier seems only to want to terrify. He seems too tangible a presence, too powerful a force to be coaxed away by prayers and offerings.

A man who claimed to have seen a lot of ghosts in his time and was not afraid of any, happened to hear of the soldier from one of my colleagues. He asked and was given permission to stay the night in one of the buildings.

The next morning, he reported that he had heard and seen nothing, but conceded that he felt a strange chill lasting for a few minutes, which could have been the duration of the ghost's visit.

The campus is strangely hushed in the evening, except for the chirping of nocturnal insects and the occasional cry of a bird; this is the time when the soldier emerges to make his rounds, although nobody sees him now or hears his heavy boots crunching the gravel outside or creaking the floorboards inside the houses.

Teng has recovered, though still pale and wan from his illness, and has settled down in another job.

Although he never talks about the soldier, he must sometimes dream of him, as Rose and I occasionally do. Never pleasant dreams these; for the hollow cough, the footsteps, the touch in the darkness, through the distorting medium of the dream, become even more terrifying.

They Do Return... But Gently Lead Them Back

Ah Cheng Peh's second wife returned even before the seventh day, in fact on the very evening after her burial in the cemetery. The sackcloth cowls of mourning were hardly removed when somebody saw her standing near the ancestral altar that held the portraits of two generations of forebears.

She was dressed as when alive – in neat long-sleeved blouse with a row of jade ornaments for buttons, sarong and embroidered slippers. She stood there saying nothing and when the person who saw her quickly signalled to the others to come and look, she was gone.

She appeared once again that evening, to a different member in the household, and everyone wondered if they had been amiss in any part of the funeral arrangements, for this return could signify displeasure. They offered joss-sticks and prayers before the altar newly set up for her, and waited to see if she would return again on the seventh day.

The floor was strewn with ashes so that if she came,

her footprints would show. Her bed was all in readiness with a clean bedsheet and pillow-cover, while on the altar were two lit candles and a pot of freshly cooked rice with a small empty bowl and a pair of delicate ivory chopsticks beside it. In the morning, the family did find the footprints in the ash, there was a hollow in the pillow where the head had lain, and when the cover of the rice pot was lifted, it was found that the cooked rice had been disturbed a little at the edges with the tips of chopsticks.

After the seventh day appearance, Ah Cheng Mm never came again, not even in dreams, to her family and relatives.

An old servant of ours, whose husband had died when she was quite young, said he too had returned on the seventh clay. The level of the water in the glass left on the altar table was considerably lower, and the two fish left with the cooked rice bore the imprint of fingers.

There were no such preparations for an uncle's return when he died, for by that time, customs such as these had been left behind. My cousins and I, with the irreverence and brashness of young people who believed that their education had made them superior to the older people around them, talked endlessly, on the night after he was buried, of ghosts and visitations from the dead. What nonsense, said one of my cousins, a young fellow who prided himself on his knowledge of science.

Superstition. Tricks of the imagination. Auto-suggestion. We were all in a light-hearted mood most unbecoming of a house of mourning, but I suppose because we were young and westernized, we were accepted with resignation by the older members in the family who, in their black clothes and sepulchral expressions, flitted about in the darkness like so many ghosts themselves.

We dredged our memories for ghost stories to share, each story becoming more outrageous than the next. Fancy embellished memory in the most extravagant manner; I remember I told one tale after another of ghost lovers, of a dead nun, of a murdered family. I told the story of my classmate in Primary one, a girl whose name I could not quite remember – was it Beng Khim? – who had died in a road accident and was seen by some, including our class teacher – actually sitting at her desk in the classroom.

The principal of a boys' school that one of my cousins attended had collapsed at his desk. He died of a heart attack on the way to hospital and soon after that a teacher, staying back to mark his pupils' exercises, heard footsteps approaching the principal's office which could be seen from the staff room. The teacher turned, saw the back of a man entering the office, and with thoughts only of nabbing a burglar or intruder, ran out to accost him. He saw no one; the door to the office was locked, and he was about to conclude that it had been the work of an over-wrought imagination, when on impulse he looked in through a small window into the office and saw, sitting at the desk and writing something on a piece of paper, the principal himself. So life-like was he – the shirt he was wearing was a favourite grey-striped one – that for a moment the teacher even forgot that he had attended his funeral only the week before, so that when he looked up, the teacher blurted out a "Good evening, Mr Chiam" with the nervous flutter of a schoolboy caught peeping. The ghost said nothing; he merely looked, unblinkingly, and it was then that the teacher was overcome by a sense of foreboding.

Making his rounds later in the evening, the school *jaga* found him in the corridor outside the office, distraught and trembling. He was incoherent for a few days and was on sick leave for a fortnight. When he recovered, he asked to be transferred to another school.

The story of the principal's ghost was hushed up by the school authorities for fear of creating fear and panic in the school, but somehow it spread, in hushed awe-stricken whispers, and a few others claimed to have seen the ghost of the principal.

A Buddhist monk was called in to perform the necessary rites of propitiation. He chanted throughout the night because the ghost was a powerful one and could only be persuaded to leave after sustained chanting of the special prayers to send it back to its home.

I remember what had struck me most about the whole incident was not the ghost's appearance itself, but the fact that a man who, with his rotundity and loud coarse jokes was the very essence of life and earthiness, had been transformed into a spirit from the next world, able to evaporate into grey mists at the crowing of the rooster.

The only time I had seen Mr Chiam was when he came to my school with some visitors; I remember him clearly because of his very loud laugh as he was talking to the principal of my school. And now he was a ghost who stalked the earth and was, unaccountably, seen only by a chosen few.

Ghosts do return, said Lau Ah Sim, the wise and pious old woman in the town of my childhood, but when they do, gently lead them back. Call them by their name, then tell them to go back quickly to their new home. If they refuse, be patient with them, and gently lead them back.

I think Lau Ah Sim must have led back lots of ghosts in her time. Her assistance was sought when the ghost of a little girl began appearing to her family and disturbing them. The child ghost did no harm, but it was said that she was continually pestering the family in one way or another, touching them, tugging at their clothes, making odd noises in their ears. One member of the family fell ill as a result, and Lau Ah Sim was called in to chant prayers and lead the ghost back.

She made a trip to the girl's grave in the cemetery, chanting prayers in her old tremulous timbre, and the ghost never did return. The little girl, in a last dream to her mother, had appeared to be asking for something. Lau Ah Sim declared that the daughter's umbilical cord had to be burnt; the mother promptly went to the cupboard where she kept her children's umbilical cords separately wrapped up in reel paper, took out the one bearing the girl's name on the outside, and burnt it.

Your daughter is now reborn, she will never pester you any more, said Lau Ah Sim.

My disbelieving cousin guffawed at the tale in great amusement, but even he must have felt uneasy that night when the dogs started howling in the darkness outside, for that meant a ghost had come. The howling was an agonized, prolonged wail and there was no full moon.

Nobody said anything, all went to sleep quietly. The howling continued and finally trailed off into a thin wail, and one of the aunts quietly got up to light a joss-stick and place it in the urn before uncle's portrait on the altar, to lead the ghost gently back.

K.C.

K.C. never told me about his rather colourful – to say the least – life in the five years I had known him. Or at least he never told me in a systematic, deliberate way. It was always the incidental mention of somebody or some incident in his conversations which led me to interrupt and say, "Rome? Monastery?" or "Did you just say your father was Wee – ? Why, you never told me!" as if a five-year friendship entitled one to know everything about one's friend.

K.C. never told anyone else though – he had a great impatience for trivia, and to him details about one's life were trivia and not worth telling. Over the years, I had pieced together whatever information I had about K.C. from himself or from the few people who knew him.

He came from a very wealthy family; his father was none other than Wee——, whose financial empire stretched from Indonesia to Hong Kong, but clearly K.C. wanted none of that wealth. His family continually struggled with his refusal to conform to their plans for him.

In his younger clays, he went off to Italy to join a monastic order, one which practised extreme asceticism: the monks slept on stone floors in tiny cells even in winter, grew their own vegetables and never once raised their eyes to look upon a female form.

K.C.'s interest in Catholicism first began while in the university, and with characteristic single-mindedness, had actually abandoned his studies in law to devote himself to a study of the faith.

The thought of a contemplative life behind the high walls of a monastery obsessed him; within months he got baptized and was on his way to Italy. The extreme regimen of life in the monastery took a severe toll on his health and he developed tuberculosis. He returned home and was nursed back to health by his parents.

In spite of his unconventional behaviour which must have been most mortifying to his conservative parents, he was much loved by them. Indeed, he was the favourite of a family of four sons and three daughters. None of the others remotely resembled him in his eccentricity; they all became professionals, successful businessmen and businesswomen in their turn.

Someone who knew his family once told me that K.C. was so uninterested in material wealth and creature comforts that he never carried money around, never bought a new shirt or tie. His mother took care of everything, unobtrusively going into his room to slip a few hundred dollars into his trouser pocket, together with a clean handkerchief.

His parents had felt that a wife would solve all their problems; a wife and children could not fail to turn him into the conventional, respectable family man they wanted him to be. They were impatient to turn over their millions to him.

Their task was made no easier by K.C.'s total indifference to women. It was neither the cultivated indifference of the superior male nor the cynicism of the misogynist; it was simply that women – at least during that period of his life – did not fit into his scheme of pleasure.

His pleasures were purely intellectual; his being naturally bashful, and his rather oversimplified view of women as fragile creatures who nevertheless possessed remarkable powers for keeping their men in a state of thrall if they wished to, kept him away from them all the while he was in the university, and made him the oddity in a campus known for its Lotharios.

His mother tried to matchmake him with a soft-spoken, decidedly genteel Indonesian Chinese girl, the daughter of a wealthy timber magnate, but the activity was all on their side for when the subject was broached, he simply burst out laughing. Mixed with all that erudition and spirituality was an irrepressible sense of humour.

Musing over a delightful piece of gossip which I had heard, I finally confronted him with it one day. He chuckled and made no attempt at denial. His resourceful mother had actually planted a beautiful woman in his room to awaken his libido, for the poor misguided parent had concluded that it was the best thing to do to interest him in women and marriage.

She waited anxiously to see the success of her efforts, and at the end of two hours, went to knock timidly on the door and ask whether they wanted any supper. K.C. was not to be found; the girl was perched prettily in one corner, patiently awaiting his return. How he had slipped out without his mother's notice she could hardly imagine.

"You were in a room with a beautiful woman and nothing happened?" I teased.

"Nothing happened," he grinned.

And yet, I suspected he was far from being the virginal ascetic-intellectual he made himself out to be. There was a period in his life – possibly after his recovery from tuberculosis when he took on a job in the Philippines – when he got involved with women. He was not particularly good-looking, being tall, stooped and skinny, but he had a charm that was irresistible, and his sense of humour, his tremendous zest for life, attracted all who met him.

I met him under rather unusual circumstances.

Being a non-driver, and hopelessly inept on the road, I had, on several occasions, fallen foul of traffic laws for pedestrians.

On one occasion, bewildered by what I perceived to be conflicting signals at a very complicated junction, I had ventured right into the middle of the junction, causing at least four vehicles to screech to an abrupt stop and at least two irate drivers to glare at me from their windows. The traffic policeman untangled the mess before motioning me to the other side of the road.

Blushing, I faced him, aware of a knot of curious onlookers. And then I had an idea. I had often been mistaken for a Japanese woman; and so, I faced the disapproving policeman who asked for my particulars in English.

I said haltingly: "I – Japanese. No *spik Englees*!" The policeman was about to close his little book and wave me on when a man stepped forward and said, in the same deliberative lilt, "She no Japanese. She Catherine Lim. *Spik Englees* and write *Englees*!"

I stared at him, and then we burst out laughing. The policeman, somewhat confused, let me off with a warning.

"How did you know me?" I asked delightedly, expecting that he would declare himself a fan.

"I read your book," he said, "In fact, I've got it here. I was curious, after the reviews, but found it disappointing."

The deflated ego of a writer does not normally admit of any politeness or friendliness, but I had been so taken in by the novelty of the situation and was at the same time so impressed by the refreshing candour of this stranger that I continued to laugh in good humour.

"But I did like the story of the old woman who dreamt of the Goddess Kuan Yin," he said, not by way of softening the severity of his earlier remark, but as a continuation of the natural flow of his thoughts.

"I had an experience akin to that once –" He paused. I quickly said, "I would love to hear about it."

"Maybe one day," he grinned before moving off, and I was disappointed that all the while he had been talking to me and waving my book about, it had never occurred to him to ask for my autograph.

I next saw K.C. in a public auditorium. I had attended a public lecture given by a visiting expert on Asian religions, and there he was sitting in the front row, listening intently. It turned out that his knowledge of Asian religions was more extensive and profound than the expert's, but this could be perceived by only a few in the audience through the drift of his questions and the substance of the comments he made.

As I was leaving the auditorium after the talk, I felt a light tap on the shoulder and turned round to see K.C. grinning and asking, "And how's the new book coming along?" I had told him, at our first meeting, I was working on another collection of short stories.

How do I explain the attraction that K.C. had for me? He has been dead these six months and I still have that sealed letter which he made me promise not to read till a year after his death, but I am convinced that it was not the attraction of a woman for a man; rather it was the compelling power of an individuality, nay, an eccentricity that stood out all the more in the midst of relentless conformity. It was the sheer power of a sense of purpose uncomplicated by considerations of wealth or public opinion; it was the love of life, the zest for knowledge and new experiences; it was above all the sparkling wit and sense of humour which was equally at home with urbane satire and earthy ribaldry.

Perhaps it was also the very unusual circumstances of his life – being born into a rich family, renouncing wealth and influence for a stint in a monastery, surviving a bout of tuberculosis to plunge into deep, philosophical studies, including Buddhism.

His life had all the trappings of a true tale of romance and must, in a city where lives predictably follow the sequence of job, marriage, family and respectability, fascinate if not captivate. Yet, looking at K.C., looking at the cheap cotton shirt, at the terribly outmoded pants, one would not invest him with any of this romantic aura.

He was always reading books and enthusiastically recommending this book or that for me. We shared an interest in literature, philosophy and the supernatural. K.C. mentioned a seance he had attended during his stay in Italy (that was when I learnt of his stint in the monastery) and that he saw what appeared to be a spirit, but was convinced there was some trickery in the whole affair.

His attitude towards the supernatural was an odd mix of cynicism and naivete; for instance, those cases of psychic phenomena that scientists had conceded were inexplicable he held with extreme skepticism, yet he was profoundly convinced that he had had three previous lives, one of which he could remember clearly.

Some people regarded him as a genius teetering on the brink of insanity; I simply found him one of the most interesting people imaginable and one with whom I could be completely at ease.

I was aware that our relationship might give rise to glib speculation. Moving easily between my world of conventional values and modes and K.C.'s maverick world where these values and modes never operated, I was conscious of some curiosity among friends about the nature of our relationship. But K.C., who had created his own world and was completely comfortable in it, was never bothered. That made for an open, uncomplicated relationship that one cherishes for life, whether with man or woman.

K.C. suddenly went abroad for some months. He wanted to see the shrines of Nepal and Bhutan, and he just packed up and left. He did ask if I wished to come along. Deeply gratified that he did not consider the presence of an inept, absent-minded and unpredictable female a hindrance, I sorrowfully declined for I had work that would occupy me for at least six months at a stretch.

K.C. returned, much thinner. The onslaught of the cancer that was to destroy him had already begun, but characteristically he told no one.

He lived in a modest rented flat, although his parents were always pestering him to return to their big house, and his mother was always trying to get him to at least come home for a meal with the family.

K.C. was not fighting his cancer in the dogged manner of a person determined to go on living. He simply did not take heed of it in his pursuit of this and that.

At the time that he collapsed and had to be taken to hospital, he was still giving lectures and was deep in research on some aspect of psychic phenomena. His sparkling wit and sense of humour remained with him till the end, and after his death, I was told of practical jokes that he had played on one of the hospital nurses.

I went to see K.C. at the hospital several times. His family had transferred him to the best private hospital, and they tolerated my presence in the hospital room only because K. C seemed so happy to see me. The cancer was spreading throughout his body; he was almost skeletal, racked continually by painful coughing. Yet there was a serenity about him that was almost reassuring.

It was hard to reconcile that I was about to lose someone whose friendship I had learnt to treasure. And once when I could no longer control my tears (it also made K.C. uneasy to see a woman cry), I walked out swiftly from the hospital room. I was around on the day of his death. He was already very weak, but was, as always, still alert.

"This is for you," he said, handing me a sealed white envelope with great effort, "and you are not to open it till a year after my death."

I took the letter sadly and then I could see that K.C. wanted to be alone; he died alone, by choice, in the large, spacious hospital room. I went home immediately afterwards, and attended his funeral and cremation the next day. His ashes were strewn over the sea, as he had wanted.

How could I not have wanted to see what was inside the sealed white envelope? I had never outgrown the childhood predilection for secrets and the tendency to be completely unsettled by the tantalizing promise of secrets not yet revealed.

This sealed letter now in my hand, from a friend on the clay of his death – it triggered off emotions at once gratifying and awesome. It was fraught with portentous possibilities – sentiments never before expressed? Some mighty secret revealed? Some insight that only people about to die were privileged to have? Some direful warning about my life? Yet there was this superstitious fear of breaking faith with the dead.

Many times had I taken out the envelope, scanned its surface for clues, even held it against the light hoping to catch some words that would provide the answer. But I saw nothing, and then it occurred to me that it could have been a huge joke being perpetrated by the irrepressible K.C.

One day, I was suddenly overcome by the desire to rip open the envelope, to put an end, once and for all, to the suspense.

I took the envelope out of the drawer; my hands trembled a little and then strangely I could not open the envelope. It may sound strange, but I could not open the envelope. My fingers seemed to have been suddenly benumbed. A sensation difficult to describe, but my hands seemed to have been independent of the rest of my body and not coordinating with it at all.

I had the curious feeling that something odd was

happening, quite independently of me. If it was indeed K.C. who was preventing me from breaking a promise to him, it was quite uncharacteristic of him.

Since then, I had only been tempted at one other time to touch the envelope, but that morning, try as I would, I could not open the drawer. It appeared stuck, although that had never happened before. I struggled with it for half an hour, then gave up. Then I tried again, and this time, it slid open easily, with the envelope lying inside.

Small signs, these; they could almost be interpreted as signs of displeasure, and I have no desire to provoke them further.

It has already been six months since K.C. died; another six months before I can open the envelope. I have never told his family, fearing, perhaps groundlessly, an attempt to break into the privacy of a communication meant only for me.